A SON RETURNS

Mohammed Khan

Copyright © 2021 Mohammed Khan

All rights reserved

The characters and events portrayed in this book are fictitious. Any similarity to real persons, living or dead, is coincidental and not intended by the author.

No part of this book may be reproduced, or stored in a retrieval system, or transmitted in any form or by any means, electronic, mechanical, photocopying, recording, or otherwise, without express written permission of the publisher.

ISBN-13: 9798469106753

Cover design by: Gabby Hafizvisur

For my Father (Abu) and Uncle (Thai Abu).
Here's to your own stories.

PROLOGUE

What was the dream I just had? I don't remember what it was, but I'm sure I was dreaming. Or was it a memory? Am I still dreaming now, or am I awake? I'm not sure. I think there was a scent of something, maybe of dry dusty earth, the scent of scorching heat. Yes that was it, and then a faint breeze approaching from the distance. I was in Pakistan, it felt like a memory from my childhood, standing in a field near my old home. My surroundings are a blur, I think there's someone calling me, I turn around and try to latch onto the voice in the distance but the person calling me is too far to know who it is. Slowly the surroundings nearest to me begin to take shape. I begin to see the houses in the distance, a farmer ploughing a field being led by a white buffalo. The constant drone of buzzing insects. Everything slowly begins to take shape, like ripples of water beginning to settle. The face calling my name is still a blur, but I can see they're dressed in white, it's a woman, her dupatta billowing behind her in the wind. I try to focus on the face in the distance but it's like they're fading further and further away.

    Linda stirred and I opened my eyes, now I know I was dreaming. A moment ago all I was hearing were those annoying bugs in the field, and that struggle to see the person's face that I just couldn't reach out to. Now it was just quiet, lying in bed facing the ceiling, listening to Linda gently dozing. Sunlight was creeping through the curtains and I remembered it was a Sunday. I felt like I should have had that feeling that comes with Sunday mornings, but I didn't. I swung out of bed and sat sideways for no real reason. Lately these dreams about Pakistan have been bugging me. Is this the mid-life crisis Wasim keeps telling me I'll end up having soon, now that I'm going to be a grandfather?

But I've been thinking about home a lot lately. *Home.* I haven't been back in over forty years and I still call it that. Linda stirred again and let out a sigh, she must have sensed I was awake. I felt like I wanted to go back to sleep but knew I couldn't.

'Why are you up so early?' she said without opening her eyes.

'Can't sleep. Do you want a tea?'

I asked the question before I even thought about it, I realised I didn't actually want one myself.

'No, you go ahead,' was thankfully her response.

She had a peculiar skill where she could tell how much effort I was willing to put into something: tea, food, even some of the bodywork I would have to do on the more peculiar dents and nicks at the garage. She could read me like a book from the things I did. I looked over my shoulder and stared at her hair as she lay facing the other direction, it was almost all grey now, but there was still the tinge of chestnut at the top that made its way to the front of her crown. Her hair was the first thing I had noticed about her the first time we met all those years ago, and then I remembered the dream I just had, and what I had lost by marrying her, and what she had given me back over the years.

'What is it?' she asked without moving.

'Nothing. Just had a bad dream.'

I got out of bed before she started asking anymore questions. As I reached the top of the stairs, I saw the outline of a burly man in a white t-shirt approach the front door through the frosted windows and drop a blue envelope through. It was the neighbour Dave from next door; he must have got one of our letters by accident again. But it was Sunday, he must have received it sometime earlier during the week, and I began to think why he waited until today to drop it off.

The blue air mail envelope was instantly recognisable, it was from Pakistan, but I hadn't received a letter from there in years. I picked it up looking for the sender's name and address but it was missing, they always put it on their letters, why did they leave it? I ripped it open to find a single sentence in Urdu in the middle of the page, my heart sank. "Your mother has died", was all it said.

'Ami?'

I dropped the letter and it landed on a field back in Pakistan. Now I saw the dream clearly, as if I could see and feel all the things around me as though there was no distance of any sort, everything was right in front of me: The farmer being pulled by the buffalo and the sound of the soil lurching from the plough underneath him, the buzzing of insects, the heat unbearably bearing down, the smell of grass, dirt, heat and dung all coming together in a heady mix, a dark skinned mother bathing her child in a nearby stream, children playing rowdily near them.

'Salim!' a voice shouted.

It was the only thing far away, the voice echoing through my mind. I turned around to the speaker, their face was no longer blurry. I looked at her face in the distance, the face I thought I would have had etched in mind for my whole life, come back to me now like a ghost. An expression of subtle anxiety was on her face, she clutched her white scarf loosely, and looked out at me with expectation, she was beckoning me. My mother, young in age, the same age I was when I left.

'Salim!' she called me.

'Salim?' said Linda as she touched me on the shoulder.

I was back home again, I wanted to say something but couldn't find the words. I just looked down at the letter on the floor, Linda hadn't noticed it at first, but she followed my gaze and went to pick it up, she looked at it quizzically.

'What does it say?' she asked.

For a moment I couldn't bring myself to say the words, but then I just pushed them through.

'My mother died'.

She looked at the letter again, perplexed as to why it only consisted of a single sentence.

'Salim, I'm so sorry'.

I was staring at the front door, not knowing what to say, what to even feel. That letter was the first sentence in Urdu I'd read in years, and of all the things it could have said. I felt lost, like a shipwrecked sailor stuck on an island. I just wanted to go home.

CHAPTER 1

1969

My story begins where it will end. Home. To a stranger's eyes it would seem like any old dustbowl in any third world country, something you'd see in a documentary, scenes played over classical Asian music coupled with a soft melancholic whine of a lonely singer. But back then whenever I'd make the daily journey back to the village from college in Lahore, I always looked out the window, as the rickety old bus wound over pot holes and dips, at the endless fields shining in the sunlight, and the simple people going about their simple lives, and I'd be thankful to God I lived out here. Here people didn't have to run around in traffic honking and screaming to get to an imaginary appointment, or having to deal with crowded streets, breathing in toxic fumes. Here, life was easy and care free, and I had the best of both worlds. I would venture out into the madness of modernity to get an education, and then every day come back to simplicity. The city boys in college would make fun of us from the country because we had no idea what they were talking about when it came to things like new music or films, or what they had watched on the one TV channel they had back then the night before. Out here in the village only one of the middle-class landlords had a TV, he had invited everyone a few weeks ago to watch the moon landing, the whole village turned out, there was so much food and commotion you'd have thought it was a wedding.

The bus came to a surging halt, my stop. Imran and I got off and made our way to our homes, along the dirt paths that lead from the main road out to the fields as we did every day. He put his hand to his hair to keep his new hairstyle intact. He had picked up a tub of Brylcreem last week after one of the city boys told him everyone was using it.

'You know they say that stuff makes you bald right?' I said, feeling sorry for someone having to make such a big deal out of their hair.

'What stuff?' he asked perplexed.

'This Brylcreem stuff you've started using.'

'Leave it *yaar*, nothing will happen. All the actors use it, you see any of them going bald? Besides we need to start looking the part in case we ever get the chance to go to England.'

Loads of men from the villages and the city were now leaving for work in the UK. Those who were already there were sending back news there was plenty of work to be found in the factories, and I had heard there were even recruitment centres being run by English people in Lahore enrolling men for work.

'Not me *yaar*, I'm staying right here with my normal haircut.'

'What? What are you talking about?' he said it almost angrily. 'Why wouldn't you want to go and work out in England, the money is so much better. You wait and see, someone's going to offer you work and you're going to run away like Fuad did.'

Fuad was a brilliant student from our village who had the potential to become a doctor or engineer, or anything else he wanted. But then his uncle sent his father an employment voucher for work in a factory, and the next thing we knew he had left for England.

'Besides *yaar*,' he carried on. 'Your mum's on her own, she needs all the help she can get.'

'I can help her right here,' I said with a hint of defiance.

'Leave it *yaar*. After we finish college, what are you going to do, go to university? That costs money, and you have to study for years before you get a degree, and you can't just do a bachelors, you'll have to do a masters, and then what? You're going to look for work? They're going to see your address on your ID card and realise you're just some village boy who doesn't know his dick from his head.'

I grimaced at the expression, another habit he'd picked up from the city boys.

'In all that time you could have gone to England, made more money than you could imagine, and bring it back for your mum with plenty to spare. No degree, no time wasting. Come back after five years you'll be the richest man in the village.'

Everyone back then had this idea, you'd go to England for a few years, make loads of money and then live the rest of your life in peace. But now I realise how naïve we all really were. For me, and all the others who moved to Britain, at some point it eventually dawned on all of us, as much as we didn't want to admit it, that we would never go back for good.

'Maybe you're right,' I said, trying to change the conversation.

'Of course I am *yaar*, you'll see it'll be for the better.'

We slowed down as I reached my house.

'You just have to promise you'll take me with you though,' pointing a finger at me.

I smiled, it was the only response I could muster.

'See you tomorrow,' he said as he raised his hand and kept on walking.

As I watched him walk on the idea of leaving home and going abroad was playing on my mind. How would all the pieces of that future fit together? How would I blend into a completely new place like England? I remember watching Goldfinger at a small cinema in a nearby town, and I remember being amazed at seeing a completely different world. Sean Connery driving a flash car in the Swiss countryside, swooning lots of different women. Of course, that was the furthest of what could have possibly been my future.

I swung the padlock hinge on the door to alert Munny I was home. Munny was the servant who had grown up with my father, but he was much more than that, he felt like a friend who was closer than family, who was always there for us. The houses in this part of the village were simple, yet relatively large for the area, ours had yellow bricks with a large steel door covered in a peeling blue paint, facing out into a field of various herbs and small vegetables. The door creaked open to reveal Munny and his beaming white smile.

'*Salaam alaikum sir gee.*'

'*Walaikum salaam.*' I responded as I walked in and he closed the creaking old door behind me.

'*Sir jee*, dinner will be a little late today, your mother has guests.'

'Who's here?'

'The tenant from Dus Chuck.'

'Ah.'

I had forgotten he was coming, the old farmer who was renting out our land in Dus Chuck village had died. Now there was a new young guy who hadn't paid his first year's rent. My mother was the only female landowner in the area, our guess was he didn't think she would be too up on keeping tabs on him, if that were the case he was about to get an unpleasant surprise.

Imran would have probably described him as someone "who didn't know their dick from their head".

'It's OK, we'll eat when Ami finishes,' I told him.

'*Teek ah.*' *OK*, he confirmed with a dip of the head.

The front door was a wicket gate that lead to a forecourt where a car could be parked, but it was empty now. It then led out into an open-air courtyard which acted as a sort of living room, the doors of the different rooms of the house surrounded this courtyard. As I made my way further in I began to hear the murmurings of the conversation that was going on. They were sat on the left side, my room was on the right, I walked past and into the room without saying anything. Best let her get on with it without prolonging anything.

'Sister you don't understand, you don't work on the land as we do,' the farmer was saying. 'The ground has been very dry since last year, and it makes –'

'Since last year?' My mother interrupted him with a steely look, lowering the cup of tea she had been drinking into her saucepan for dramatic effect. 'Ironic how the land decides to dry up as soon you move in.'

The farmer gave a shy laugh and was about to offer a further explanation before she continued.

'The tenants in Barapa managed to pay their rent on time, just as they do every year,' Barapa was the village next to Dus Chuck where she also owned land. 'But here you are saying *your* ground is dry.'

I took my books out slowly onto the desk, watching the conversation through the wire meshing on the door that acted as a window.

'No sister, you see in Barapa they just had a new irrigation system installed, that's why-'

'Do you really take me for some idiot?' She put the cup

and saucer down onto the table sharply. My mother's bluntness forced his face to drop its shy smile. 'I went there last week myself to meet with the tenant in Barapa and there is no new irrigation system there. The stingy old man who keeps the land there even refuses to buy a tractor even when I offer to buy one for him, he's still getting pulled around by that sickly buffalo that's as old as he is! He doesn't do anything to the land without asking me first. He's too scared to do anything on his own initiative, even though he's been there since before partition and knows the land better than anyone.'

The farmer lowered his eyes to the ground, he wasn't used to being shouted at by a woman.

'I've heard the rumours about you, and frankly it's none of my business. But if you want to keep your livelihood I suggest you clean yourself up and get back to what you're supposed to be doing.'

The tenant in Barapa had told Ami that this guy was just lying around getting drunk all day.

'Do you understand?'

'*Jee maam.*' Yes ma'am.

'Now you haven't brought the rent for this year. You have six months to bring me a year and half's rent.'

He raised his head to protest and say something, but she raised her hand to stop him.

'I have no problem with any of my other tenants. Ali, may God forgive him, was an honourable man, he looked after the land you have now before he passed away, and he would always pay the rent. If occasionally he couldn't pay it on time, he would be honest and tell me in advance, inviting me to see for myself if there were any problems. He wouldn't come to me a month after the rent was due and make up some silly excuse that would make it obvious he was lying. Have I made myself clear to you?'

'*Jee maam.*'

'Don't take me as a *zameendar* that just sits around all day waiting for the rent to come in and know nothing about how the land is cultivated.'

'No, no, it's not like that *maam*,' he said with his shy smile returning, 'It's just that-'

'No more excuses,' her expression had changed to one of sympathy and her tone softened. 'Have I made myself clear?'

He nodded his head, eyes lowered.

'Then go.'

He made his way to leave, Munny followed him out with one of his rare stern expressions. Once he was out of sight and the metal gate had opened and closed for him, I came out into the courtyard. Ami relaxed her body now that her telling off was over.

'How are you son?' she said as I approached, her tired expression remaining. Her white dupatta hung loosely from her hair, she wore a light turquoise shalwaar kameez. 'How was college?'

'Fine. How was your day?'

She scoffed and motioned to the door with her head.

'These young men are so frustrating to deal with. At least with the old men they don't have the energy to make up excuses.'

We both smiled, and then the seriousness returned, though this time it was something different. She paused for a moment, she wanted to say something but was hesitant.

'Salim, I want to talk to you about something,' she finally managed. She picked up a letter from the mango wood table to her side. 'I was hoping to talk to you about it later, but now might be better before your brother gets home. I got a letter from Mawlana Ahmed today. Do you remember him?'

'Of course.' The mention of his name brought his wide toothy smile, big bushy beard and gleaming eyes to mind. He was a friend of my father's since they were children. He was the one *molvi*, religious scholar, in the village who didn't beat his madrassa students, shortly after dad had died and I had finished learning how to read the Qur'an with him he had moved to England for work.

'He says they are looking for workers in his factory in London. He says they take anyone sixteen and above, and wants to know if you would like to go.'

I stayed silent for a moment not sure what to say.

'What do you think?' I asked her.

'I want you to study,' she put it bluntly, but then her face softened. 'But I know work in England is rewarding, a simple factory job there sometimes pays much better than a good professional job here, at least that's what I'm told. If it were up to me I wouldn't have mentioned it, but Mawlana Ahmed asked me so I felt obliged to tell you.'

How ironic was it that I just had this conversation with Imran, and now all of a sudden this comes out of nowhere? The thought of leaving made my stomach lurch. If Imran could see into my head he would have thought I was crazy for not saying yes straight away. But to leave Ami, my brother, my home, college, all my friends to go live in another country when I hadn't even been further than Lahore, it was all a bit much for a seventeen-year-old.

'I want to study too. But if you need the money-'

'I don't need the money. I want my sons with me.'

She breathed a deep sigh and looked at the letter as if searching for something.

Munny opened the creaking front door, Abbas, my younger brother, came running through, a flash of white in his bright uniform. I hadn't even heard him knock.

'*Salaam alaikum* mummy!' he squealed as he ran to hug her.

'*Walaikum salaam* son,' she put the letter back in its envelope and to the side as he came up to her. 'How was school?'

'*Teek*.' Fine.

'Good, *Allah ka shukr hai*' Thanks be to God. 'Go change your clothes, Munny is about to get dinner ready,' With that he sped off towards the door behind me that lead to his room, she watched him with a hint of sadness 'Don't tell him about the letter, he'll be heartbroken. Think about it and tell me what you think.'

* * *

I lay in bed that night, darkness surrounding me, hands behind my head, the ceiling fan above me whirling away. It felt like a record being played and every half second there was a break in the music to be replaced with the chirp of crickets outside. The cacophony of the two sounds felt like it was digging into my mind.

England. What did I know about it? James Bond comes from England, he has loads of girlfriends, does everyone in England have girlfriends? Would I be able to have a girlfriend if I was away from home? No, Mawlana Ahmed would make sure that wouldn't happen, he'd probably send me back straight away. Would he send me back on a plane? What are planes like? I've never been in one before. What are the people in England like? In films they always seem polite and kind and dignified. Yeah, the people must be nice.

I sat up in bed, all of these dissonant thoughts running around in my mind. I was asking the wrong questions I told myself. I shouldn't be thinking about what England is like, I should be thinking about what leaving home is like. What would it feel like to be away from Ami, Abbas, Munny, Imran. Not being able to come home at the end of the day, to not be able to see your family and friends.

Ami had said she didn't need the money. Was she not being honest? She was chasing up the tenant from Dus Chuck today, she had been chasing up other tenants on their rent as well recently. If she didn't want me to go she could have just not mentioned the letter and I wouldn't have been none the wiser. But she did. Ami was the kind of person who would never admit they need money or have any financial problems, she was too proud, and sometimes, a bit too stubborn. I convinced myself that must be why she asked me if I was interested in going. She was always keen for me and Abbas to study and get degrees, this offer of sending me to work in England was completely out of character. That must be it. There could be no other explanation.

I lied back down again feeling a little relieved. Why, I wasn't entirely sure. Maybe because in my mind it now made sense to take Mawlana Ahmed up on his offer. If I can work there for a few years and come back with some cash saved, I can give it to Ami and then hopefully go back to studying. And I wouldn't need to bring it up with her.

If only I had known then what I know now. How naïve and foolish I was. But then again, I was young, I didn't know better. If I could go back and tell myself what would become of me, would the young me even believe me? I suppose the one thing that would have been the most unthinkable, was the fact that I would never come back for good.

❊ ❊ ❊

The bus ebbed and flowed along the road towards Lahore, the same scenes played out on the fields repeating themselves every day, but today was different in a way. Imran talked nonchalantly next to me as I stared out the window.

'What's up with you today?'

'Huh, what?'

His question took me by surprise.

'What's up with you? You're just staring out the window.'

'I always stare out the window.'

'Yeah but at least you say something that lets me know you're not dead.'

I was hoping my feelings wouldn't betray me, turned out I trusted them too easily. There was nothing I could do, he put me into a corner and now I was forced to tell him the inevitable.

'Ami got a letter from Mawlana Ahmed yesterday.'

'He's not dead is he?!'

'How could he send a letter if he was dead?'

'Oh yeah.'

'Anyway, you *befcoof*, he wrote a letter,' I had to take a breath hoping I'd have time to find the right words. 'Asking me to come to England.'

'What?!'

Some of the other boys turned to look at him and I felt a rush of embarrassment. I was hoping to tell him gently so he wouldn't overreact like he does when he gets excited. Turns out my emotions let me down again.

'We were just talking about it yesterday! You're going right?'

'Yeah I think so.'

'I knew it! I knew if you had the opportunity you'd pack your bags and go.'

'What's going on *yaar*?' The boy sitting across from the aisle asked Imran. I moved my hand to put onto his arm to get him to stop but it was too late.

'This prick is leaving us to go party in England.'

'Eh? To party?' he was a little confused. 'I thought people go to England to work.'

'*Han han* that's what they tell you, but they spend more time drinking beer in pubs and chasing white girls.'

The other boy bobbed his head in approval with a wide smirk across his face. I became incredulous, all of a sudden Imran was on a high.

'What's wrong with you? Where are you getting all this from?'

He had an evil but joking smile on his face.

'Hey if you're going to take my idea and leave without me I'm going to make sure you leave without any sense of honour attached to your name.'

While these rare outbursts of sarcasm were getting rarer for him as he was getting older, they still hadn't disappeared completely.

'Seriously though,' he said slightly sombrely now. 'It's good you have this opportunity, make the most of it.'

'I will. And if there's an opportunity for you I'll let you know. I can't promise the other stuff though.'

'It's fine, you would be useless with women anyway.'

CHAPTER 2

Present

I hate rummaging through boxes. Like our memories, we stuff our old possessions into a corner to make space for what we think is important. It's only when we take them out again we realise how much they meant to us to begin with.

In the dimness of our attic I realised my eyes aren't what they used to be. I was struggling to see what each thing was, but eventually I found the one large box shaped object I was looking for. Peeling off the dusty old sheet used as a cover I finally felt the relief that comes when you finally find something you're desperately searching for. The old trunk I had to come to the UK with. I poured the things I thought that were important to me when I left Pakistan into this, little did I realise that I had poured my old life into it.

As I began to rummage through, the memory I had for each thing would unlock itself as I picked it up to look at it. Everything was faded and grey, like the pieces of an old black and white movie: My green Pakistani passport, the brown suit I was wearing when I arrived here, an old gold watch that belonged to my father that had stopped ticking long ago. Eventually I found the one thing I came looking for, my old photo album. It creaked open as I gently flipped the hardback cover, more memories I had forgotten about. One of the first photos was of me and my housemates who I worked with at the Ford factory. I remembered it was one of our rare days off, the four of us standing outside in suits, 60's cars parked on the roads, everyone had front gardens and no driveways back then. Another photo was of me and Linda in a bar in Soho, young and carefree, I was still wearing the same old suit surrounded by white people in more colourful attire. As I turned the pages glimpses of my life kept coming back to me, but there was only one thing I wanted to think about, I eventually found it on the last page. It was a picture of me and Ami, standing outside our house, the fields winding away in the back. The day I left Pakistan. Her with her usual stoic expression, draped in her dupatta, and me pensive about my impending journey.

I wanted to cry, my insides lurched, I wanted to set myself free from all this emotion, but for some reason I just couldn't. I looked down at her face and her gaze peering straight at me, a wave of sadness washed over me and eventually a tear let itself go. It was a small respite, I wanted to scream, but I couldn't and I knew it wouldn't achieve anything, it wouldn't bring her back after I had forgotten all about her.

I heard Linda's steps as she came upstairs, I quickly wiped away the tear so she wouldn't see it and put the photo to the side and started putting everything else away.

'What are you looking for up here Salim?' she asked as she came closer.

I passed her the photo of Ami without saying anything and then carried on packing the trunk.

'Oh wow, I don't think I've ever seen this photo. You look so young and innocent'. We smiled together, it was a welcome relief.

'What else have you managed to dig out?' she asked me.

'Just some more old memories, broken watches and expired passports. You know this is the trunk I came to this country with?'

'Yes dear, you tell me that every time you go rummaging through it.'

'When was the last time?'

'Oh,' neither of us realised how long it had been. 'Must have been more than twenty years ago now, when we moved house and you came across it. I didn't realise it was so long ago.'

There was an awkward silence as we both reflected on how much time had passed us by without us realising.

'Salim, what are you going to do?'

It was a vague question, I looked up at her to find an explanation.

'What do you mean?'

'I mean, now that your mum's died, what are you going to do? Aren't you going to call your brother or something?'

I should have called him as soon as the letter arrived, but I was afraid he wouldn't want to talk to me. Things weren't exactly great between us. But then again it must have been him who sent the letter. I suddenly felt disappointed that all he could send me were four words, he couldn't even tell me that she was sick or dying.

'Yeah I should. I'm just a little upset he didn't call himself.'

'Does he even have our number? Thinking about it, you haven't been in contact with them for years, how did he even have our address?'

'I was sending mum money every few months.'

'What?' It sounded like she wanted to be incredulous, but it came out half-heartedly. 'You never mentioned that to me.'

Any other day I would have asked why I had to tell her everything, but not today.

'I know, I'm sorry. I should have told you.'

'It's alright. I guess it's not that a big deal,' she paused a moment, as though she had to calm herself for not making a fuss. 'You should come downstairs you've been up here all morning.'

'Yeah I will.'

She made her way to go back downstairs.

'You will call him won't you? Your brother.'

'Yes dear.'

She descended down the stairs each step creaking as she stepped off it. I carried on going through my old possessions to lose myself in my thoughts once more. But I didn't really know what I was doing, or what I was looking for. After all these years would a simple phone call really be enough? Was calling Abbas all I could do?

I stared at the photo of me and Ami outside the house, the fields behind us. For a moment it felt like I could feel the wind and the heat from that day, it felt good to be back there, back with her.

I sat down in an old leather office chair, it let out a long creak as I leaned back. It was clear now, and almost felt inevitable. I'd decided a phone call definitely wasn't enough. I needed to go back.

CHAPTER 3

1969

I looked at myself in the mirror and tried to adjust the blazer I was wearing, but to be honest, I didn't how these things were meant to fit. How did English people wear these? I had it on for less than five minutes and I already hated it. I was used to wearing shalwaar kameez nearly all the time, going to school and college we'd wear shirt and trousers, but they would be loose and cotton, this brown wool suit mum had bought me just felt weird, and I felt extra hot wearing it. I could feel the sweat profusing from my forehead.

Then a thought crossed my mind: everyone in England wears these; in Pakistan all the well-to-do people did too, businessmen, doctors, professors. With this in mind I decided to take another look at myself in the mirror, straightened my back and pulled the blazer down to make it fit tighter, which had no effect, but for whatever reason my young mind decided, *now* I look good.

I picked up my trunk by its leather handle, heavy with all the things I could take with me, mostly clothes, but mum had decided to give me a whole kitchen's worth of herbs and spices, and all the varieties of daal I had space for. "You might not be able to get our food over there, you don't want to end up having to eat their pork," is what she said. I didn't know any better so

I didn't disagree with her. I opened the door and the sun bore down heavily, it was mid-morning and the heat was beginning to pick up, I felt it more with the unfamiliar suit on. Mum and Abbas were standing waiting expectedly, a look of apprehension on their faces. Munny was waiting near the front door, he had borrowed his brother's car to take me to the airport, it felt like even the car was waiting for me as its engine slowly chugged away.

'*Mashallah, mashallah,*' Ami said as she walked forward to straighten the lapels and brush my shoulders. 'My son hasn't even left and he's already a full-blown Englishman,' we both smiled together. 'Remember to write often.'

'OK.'

'If you have any problems talk to Mawlana Ahmed.'

'OK.'

'He's going to pick you up from the airport.'

'I know.'

'And-'

'Ami, it's fine. I know.'

She pursed her lips slightly, it's what she would do when she was annoyed at something, but knew it was better not to say anything.

'*Acha*,' OK. 'You better get going you don't want to miss your flight.'

'One minute,' Munny interrupted. 'Let's take a photo.'

He was holding a camera in his hands, its strap around his neck.

'Where did you get that from?' I asked.

'It was in the car *sir gee*, it's my brother's.'

Mum positioned herself next to me and fixed her usual

white duppata hanging loosely over her hair. Munny squinted through the viewfinder, and he shook his head.

'No, there's too many shadows here,' he waved his hand around. 'Let's go outside where it's brighter, I'll turn the flash on so it becomes even better.'

Of course, back then none us knew the flash made no difference during the day.

We made our way outside and stood in front of the fields, the hot sun bearing down on us. She waved her hand at Abbas to beckon him.

'Come here Abbas, let's take a photo,' Ami said to him.

He shook his head vigorously.

'Don't be silly! Come on.'

'I don't want to,' he was pouting now, with his lower lip jutting out, he was on the verge of tears.

'*Chalo*, as you wish,' she didn't want to upset him further, on any other day she would have insisted until he gave in. We stared at the camera as Munny again squinted into the viewfinder.

'*Vun, too, three!*' The camera clicked, the flash was hardly visible. Munny bobbed his head in approval of his work. '*Chalo chiliye sir gee*,' come on let's go.

Mum turned and hugged me, I hugged her back.

'Look after yourself son,' she let go and turned to Abbas. 'Say bye to your brother.'

He sensed the finality of the moment and his tears finally released themselves. He tried to hide them as he came forward and hugged my leg, he was still too short then to hug me properly. I put my hand on his back in return, unsure of what to say to him. Munny started to roll the car back out of the forecourt, I tried to move forwards but Abbas hadn't loosened his grip.

'Come on Abbas, I have to go.'

'Don't go,' came his muffled response.

Mum moved forward and gently loosened his grip.

'Salim will be back soon *beta*. He's only gone for a little while. When he comes back you won't even realise he had left.'

Abbas wiped the tears from his eyes, seemingly to be comforted by what she said to him.

As I went to place my trunk in the boot, Imran arrived with a sly smile on his face.

'Who's this white guy going back to England?'

'Would it make you happy if I told you I was sorry?'

'No,' his smile widened. 'First thing you need me to do is find me a job, then a girlfriend and a house, once you have that sorted you can post me a ticket.'

'I'll try, but I can't make any promises.'

We shook hands, and his smile was replaced with a look of solemnity.

'Look after yourself.'

'You too.' I wanted to hug him as a way of saying goodbye, but it just wasn't thing for two men to do in Pakistan. Men only hugged on Eid day, and even then it was a solemn affair. I was already feeling bad for not knowing how to bid farewell to Abbas, now I felt more embarrassed that I couldn't do anything more for Imran either.

I turned around and finished putting my trunk in. As I sat into the dusty front seat next to Munny, Ami and Abbas stood next to Imran. As I rolled down the window I tried to hold back my emotions so I wouldn't feel the urge to cry. A part of me just wanted this moment not to happen, to be able to just stay at home and sleep in my bed that night, to wake up the next morning and just go to college with Imran, not to have to face this uncertainty before me. I could just stay here and not have to worry about all the new things I now had to deal with. I had never been on a flight before, never been to another country, I was about to enter a whole new world that I knew nothing about. But I couldn't back out now, it was too late to change my mind, I just had to close my eyes and force myself to jump into the sea I was standing over.

As the car pulled away from the house I waved to them as they disappeared into the distance. I looked out at the fields as they passed us by, felt the wind bring the smells of the village to my nostrils. I wondered if England smelt like this, does the sun feel the same way as it does here? Or are no two places in the world the same? Is that a way for God to tie your memories to a place? Forbidding any other place on the Earth to share the sights, sounds and smells of another?

Now I think back to that moment, I realise it changed my life forever and I unwittingly left a part of myself there. Sometimes I would come across a smell or a sound that would remind me of the village; the smell of a diesel engine grinding itself would be like that of a rickshaw. Sometimes a gutter would get blocked when it rained heavily and it would remind me of the open gutters in the village running alongside the edge of the houses. Vile to most, to me it was the smell of my childhood.

No, two places are never the same. God lets them share pieces of one another so that when we move from one to the next we're reminded of where we came from or we've been. But they're never the same.

CHAPTER 4

1969

The first thing I remember about getting off the plane in England was the damn cold. It was biting and freezing, I had never experienced anything like it before. It was made worse by the fact I didn't have an overcoat, and I hadn't been able to sleep on the flight. I remember standing in the queue for immigration, unable to shake the feeling of cold even after coming inside. After a few steps I would end up under a vent that would blow out hot dry air, but rather than making me feel warm it would just make my tired eyes feel irritated.

I took a moment out of my despair to look around me. As I had come off a PIA flight most of the people immediately around me were Pakistani, but most of the people waiting in the lines were English, it was a little unnerving to be surrounded by people who looked completely different to me. I suppose I better get used to it I thought to myself.

'Next!'

Awoken from my daydreaming I stumbled forward.

'Hello sir,' the immigration officer said as he took my passport. 'Are you here on a work visa?'

He had a bushy blonde moustache, I wasn't used to hearing English being spoken so fast, even that short sentence I had to break down in my head before mustering a response.

'Ah yes,' I responded. Hoping I had answered correctly.

He flicked through the blank green pages until it landed on my work permit.

'The Ford factory? It's quite popular these days, sometimes most of what I get is Ford, other days all I seem to get is everything but Ford!"

He let out a loud chuckle which reverberated around his mouth. I nodded my head in agreement, though I wasn't sure what he said. His accent was nothing like what I was used to hearing.

He finished flicking through the rest of the passport and reached for his stamp.

'Everything's in order,' he banged his stamp into the passport. 'Enjoy your stay in England Mr Khan.'

Still not knowing what he said, I assumed that by stamping and giving me back my passport meant that I could go.

'Thank you,' I said nodding, unsure of myself. I moved away slowly in case there was something else.

I made my way to baggage reclaim, collected my trunk and exited through the doors, it felt like I had entered a new world. Everything was clean and shiny, it felt so far away from Pakistan, not just in terms of distance, but the way it looked and felt. Everything seemed like it was made out of metal and the whole place was covered with artificial white light. It was a stark contrast from the magnolia colour paint and natural light at Lahore Airport.

I looked around to find a familiar face. Mawlana Ahmed had said he would pick me up from the airport, but given he had been living in England for a few years now I would have thought he would have got rid of the big bushy beard and started wearing English clothes, I didn't know how I would recognise him so I half waited for a familiar voice to ring out.

'Salim! Over here!' I heard a voice shout in Punjabi.

I looked over to my right, and there standing a few feet away was the exact same Mawlana Ahmed I remembered, bushy beard, shalwaar kameez, white turban, he hadn't changed a bit, apart from the big grey overcoat he was wearing, and he had wrapped his green shawl around his neck to keep out the cold.

'How are you? How was the flight?' He shook my hand vigorously in his.

'Fine, fine,' I muttered.

I was a little taken aback, not only was I cold and sleep deprived in a completely foreign and weird place, but all of a sudden I was confronted with one of the most familiar faces from my childhood. It was all a bit too much. It also didn't help that quite a few people were discreetly staring at Mawlana's appearance, in a way I would eventually learn was the English way of staring at things.

'Good, good! Here let me take your luggage. The van is outside.'

Before I could offer the customary refusal he had picked it up and was on his way.

Heading back outside into the cold biting wind, it didn't feel as bad as when I had stepped off the plane. It was still bad, just not as bad. Maybe it had felt worse before because the open space of the runway provided no protection from the wind. We reached Mawlana's worn out white van, it had tinges of rust around the wheels and on parts of the body. He put the trunk into the back which had benches on either side and nothing else, and we clambered in.

'You've already made your first mistake,' he said, as he began to whir the old thing to life.

'What's that?' I asked him quizzically.

'You didn't bring a coat. It's OK everyone who comes here in the winter makes that mistake, here take mine.'

He proceeded to take off his big grey overcoat, I began to protest.

'No, no, it's OK uncle, I'll buy one.'

'Listen *yaar*, how much money did you bring with you?'

'Err, £5, it's all they allow.'

'Exactly, a decent winter coat costs at least ten.'

I gawked at what he said, £10 for a coat? For that much money I could live and eat in the village in Pakistan for weeks.

'Take my coat and you can give it back to me when you get your own.'

'OK,' I took it with both a sense a relief and reluctance.

He began to move the van slowly out of the space and then proceeded to the series of turns and bends that lead to the bottom of the car park. It was my first time in a multi-storey car park and it felt so weird spinning round the long downward ramp. The ramparts on either side felt like they were so close they would scrape the van at any point.

'Does everything cost so much here?' I asked him.

'Oh no, just the stuff that matters!' He said laughing. 'Don't worry *yaar* everyone who comes here fresh has to go through these problems: Money, the cold, oh and by the way there's starting to be a little commotion about all the people coming here for work, a lot of people don't like us being here, but don't worry just pray for them.'

It was a typical Mawlana Ahmed statement.

'Why don't they like us?'

'Because we're foreigners in their country. Never mind they were in ours for 400 years, as soon as we come over to work in their factories, all of a sudden they don't like us anymore! Don't worry you'll be fine. Just put your trust in Allah and you'll be fine.'

I wondered why this was one of the first things he felt the need to mention to me. I tried to put it to the back of my mind.

I had read stories about Sufis and Qalanders, the wandering dervishes, and the amazing tales about their character and miracles they used to produce. Whenever I read those stories they always reminded me of Mawlana Ahmed, though I always just thought of them as fictional stories that were meant to provide some sort of life lesson. Some of the stories about the dervishes used to say they were "drunk on the wine of divine love", Mawlana Ahmed's boisterous character and appearance fitted the description perfectly. Nothing could faze him or make him look down on anything. He planted a seed of doubt as to whether they were made up stories or not.

'How was the food on the plane?' he asked.

'Terrible.'

'Of course it was! English food is the worst. Don't bother with it! Stick to our roti and salan you'll be fine. I told one of the guys you're staying with to make something for you when we arrive.'

'Where *am* I staying?' The question hadn't even crossed my mind until now.

'There's a house with other guys who work in the Ford factory with me, you'll share it with them. They are good people *mashallah*. There's one Indian Hindu, but don't worry he's OK, he'll be Muslim soon inshallah,' he said jokingly.

'Indian?' I asked him.

'Yeah, yeah don't worry, leave that partition animosity back home! Everyone is equal here.'

Mawlana Ahmed's usual sense of tranquillity over all

things failed to have an effect on me this time. The 1965 war was still fresh in my memory, having to share a house with the "enemy" didn't really sit well with me, and I think Mawlana Ahmed sensed it.

'Don't worry Ranjit has been here since before the war. He's not a spy or a soldier!'

He let out another boisterous laugh. Another thing I tried to put it to the back of my head, seemed like I had plenty of things to worry about.

As we went further away from Heathrow and closer towards Central London I slowly noticed the houses and buildings become larger and fancier. I looked out of the window and wondered what kind of place I would be staying in.

'Salim look! That's Big Ben!'

I leaned forward to look up at the massive clock tower I had seen in so many pictures towering above us.

'Are you allowed to go inside?' I asked.

'Oh yes, well you go inside the parliament, you can't go up the clock tower, and you have to get a ticket anyway, not like this government takes enough tax. On the right is the River Thames.'

I looked to the other side as we weaved our way around Parliament Square.

'It's brown,' I said rather disheartened.

'Yeah, I don't know why, I would have thought they would have paid to make it clear, but who knows!'

I still couldn't get over how different everything looked. There were people walking their dogs, families out for a day trip, tourists taking pictures. And though the traffic was busy, it was so quiet, no one was using their car horn. A busy road in Pakistan meant you would hear horns blaring all day, but here it was so quiet and it felt like everyone knew which way everyone else was going.

'This is the Tower of London,' he pointed out to the right as we stopped at the traffic lights. 'It's where the Queen keeps the Kohi Noor her grandmother stole from us.'

'I suppose you can't go there then.'

'Oh yes you can. But again you have to get a ticket. Can you believe that? They charge you money and take your wealth, to see the wealth they stole! Hmph!'

As we carried on further and further, slowly the big fancy buildings started turning into factories. I began to see other people who looked like me but at the same time were different: Bengalis, Sikhs with their turbans, Indian women wearing wool coats on top of their saris.

'Who are these people Mawlana?'

I pointed to a group of men with big beards dressed in black, they looked like white Muslims.

'Jews.'

I had never seen Jews before, but then again I hadn't seen many Sikhs or Hindus either. I'd see them sometimes here and there in Lahore but it felt like there were more of them here in England. In one instance it felt like I was still in a strange new place, I was used to seeing only one facet of the sub-continent in Pakistan, but at the same time these people had more in common with me than the English people I saw at the airport, even if I did consider them to be different.

Eventually Mawlana turned down a side road of small terraced houses and brought his old van to a screeching stop, applying the squeaky hand brake.

'Here we are! Home sweet home!'

I got out of the car and took a look at my new home, it couldn't be any more different to the house in the village. But then I realised this house also had yellow bricks and a blue door. God's way of being ironic maybe?

Mawlana took my trunk out of the boot before I could even offer to take it from him as I was still staring up at the house. Before I realised he was already opening the front door.

I was greeted by the familiar smell of curry being cooked, it brought with it a tinge of sadness as it reminded me of home, which was now so far away. But before the feeling could settle Mawlana ushered me forward through the narrow corridor.

'*Ajo, ajo,*' *come on.*

He opened the kitchen door, three men were sitting around a tiny kitchen table smoking, another was standing over a boiling pot on the stove.

'*Asalaam alaikum!*' Mawlana greeted them boisterously.

'*Walaikum salaam!*' Came their equally boisterous response.

'*Astaghfirullah!*' Mawlana pointed to the ashtray as he put my trunk down. It was filled to the brim, almost to the point the butts were about to fall onto the kitchen table. 'You should be ashamed of yourselves! Smoking so much, this is no way to start off with our new guest.'

He had switched to talking in Urdu, so I assumed this was a mixed group of Pakistanis.

'*Maulvi saab,*' said one of the men sitting on the table, blowing out smoke. 'He's a young man, if he doesn't already smoke as much as we do, he will soon enough!'

The rest of them laughed gleefully.

'*Khabaar daar,*' *don't you dare.* 'His father was a good friend of mine and I don't want him picking up any bad habits while he's here. Otherwise his mother will never forgive me.'

'OK *maulvi saab*, don't worry,' said the man stirring the pot at the stove. He exuded a sense of calmness and responsibility. 'We'll look after him.'

'*Chalo,*' *good*. He indicated towards me, 'This is our new guest, Salim.'

They stood up to greet me, the man at the stove wiped his hands and moved forward too. Mawlana began to introduce each of them, I shook each person's hand and gave them salaam.

'This is Humayun, and Tariq, and Tahir,' he pointed to each one of them in turn, they were the ones sitting around the table. 'And this is our resident Hindu, Ranjit,' he said pointing to the one approaching from the stove.

I tried not to look like I was caught surprised, but as I looked at him closer his sharp features made him stand out from the rest of them, he looked like an intelligent man, not someone I would expect to be working in factories, he looked like someone who should have been a university professor or a doctor.

'How do you do?' I asked him in my heavily accented English, I wasn't really sure what to say to him, I couldn't really greet him with a salaam.

'Fine, jolly good,' he responded also in a heavy accent with a warm smile as he reciprocated my handshake with a warm, firm grip.

'Ranjit is also the chef,' said Mawlana Ahmed. 'But he is a vegetarian, so if you want to eat meat you will have to cook it yourself. All these other bums are too busy to do it themselves, so they've pretty much become vegetarian too.'

'Mawlana, his rice and daal is superb, we don't need to eat meat anymore,' said Humayun, the other two laughed.

'See what I mean,' said Mawlana. 'They'd rather forgo meat than have to cook it. There's a Bengali halal butcher down the road on Commercial Street -'

'Mawlana saab!' interjected Ranjit as he walked back to the

stove. 'Let him settle down a bit and then he can worry about getting his meat intake. I'm sure he'll be fine with rice and daal for today at least.'

I had forgotten how hungry I actually was, the thought of eating what was currently filling the house with aroma sounded really appealing after the abysmal meal on the flight.

'*Chalo teek hain*,' *OK then*, Mawlana agreed. 'I'm going to go now, I'll see you all in the morning,' he looked towards me, I didn't realise he wasn't staying with us, I was a little disheartened, he was the only person I really knew here. 'Salim, I make the rounds to pick up the men for the factory at 6, be ready nice and early OK?'

I nodded in agreement.

'*Chalo teek hain*,' he repeated and turned to leave. '*Salaam alaikum*'.

'*Walaikum salaam*,' we all responded in unison, though not as a loud as before. With that he left and here I was left with a group of strangers in a new home.

'Hope you're hungry,' said Ranjit.

'Very,' I replied.

'Good, have a seat, it'll be ready soon.'

Tahir took out a spare chair from under the table, I wasn't sure how there was even space for it. I squeezed in amongst them.

'Cigarette?' asked Tariq.

'I don't smoke.'

'Ah, mummy's boy eh?' said Humayun with a smile and tap on the shoulder. 'Don't worry we were all young mummy's boys when we first came here. Now we all smoke!'

The room erupted in laughter, I just about managed to

smile.

'Don't worry,' said Tahir. 'Things seem strange now, but once you've had some food, got some sleep, had your first day at work. Things will fall in place *inshallah*, you'll get used to everything.'

I appreciated the advice he had to give, I was still feeling a little awkward being in a tiny kitchen surrounded by older men I had only just met. But that simple bit of advice made feel a little better.

'*Inshallah*,' I replied.

'So what's your story?' asked Tariq as he tapped his cigarette in the ashtray.

'My story?'

'Where are you from?' explained Tahir. 'And where are you going?'

I wasn't sure if it was meant to be such a profound question. It certainly sounded like it.

'I'm from a village near Lahore, I was studying English literature at college before Mawlana found work for me.'

'Educated man,' Humayun said turning to Ranjit. 'Just like you!'

'More brains to work for the white men's factories,' Ranjit said sombrely. He was rinsing out rice he had left to soak, getting ready to boil it.

'Where are you guys from?' I asked them collectively.

'Me and Tariq are also from Punjab,' explained Tahir. 'He's from Gujranwala, I'm from Sialkot. Same place Ranjit was from before partition, before his family moved to Delhi. For a smart guy his Punjabi is terrible.'

Ranjit let out a snicker.

'Humayun over here is from Karachi,' carried on Tahir. 'So because of these two,' he indicated to Ranjit and Humayun. 'We're only allowed to speak Urdu in the house.'

'Damn right!' Humayun exclaimed enthusiastically. 'I hate hearing that village language, "*kitey, kida, uda vich*". Urdu is the real language of Pakistan, the language of poets!'

He twisted his hand for dramatic effect.

'Go on then,' Tariq turned to him. 'Give us some poetry.'

Humayun's face became flabbergasted. Almost as if he had been asked a really embarrassing question.

'There's that poem from Iqbal, or is it Bulleh Shah?'

'Bulleh Shah's poetry was in Punjabi *befcoof*!' Tahir raised his voice at him slightly. 'I thought you didn't like that "village language".'

'Yeah, of course,' Humayun tried to brush it off. 'I meant Ghalib, not Bulleh Shah.'

'Better than the entire world is our India,' Ranjit interjected calmly. 'We are its nightingales and it is our garden.'

'*Yaar* spare us your propaganda songs,' Humayun said to him shaking his head with a wince.

Tahir leaned forward and hit Humayun on the back of the head. Not sure who it took more by surprise, him or me. Tariq and Ranjit were unfazed.

'That's Allama Iqbal you *bhenchod* have some respect.'

'Allama Iqbal wrote poetry about India?' Humayun rubbed the back of his head. 'I thought he was Pakistani?'

Tariq and Tahir both clicked their tongues and shook their head in disgust.

'He passed away before partition,' Tariq said. 'What do they teach kids in Karachi eh?'

'If we are in a foreign place,' I continued the poem. 'The heart remains in the homeland, for that is the only place it can truly belong.'

'*Vah, vah,*' Tariq and Tahir both said in unison, pointing at me with their palms open and raised. It was the standard response to when hearing poetry in Pakistan.

'Here you go Ranjit,' Tahir shouted to him. 'You have a fellow poet you can perform a *mushaira* with.'

He snickered again.

'I'm surprised they even teach you that poem in school,' said Ranjit.

'I read it outside of school,' I said.

'Ah,' he turned off the hob and picked up the pot with a tea towel on the handles. 'That explains it. In India we consider it our second national anthem. Some even prefer it over the real one.' He placed it on the table and then went back to get the daal.

I started thinking about the words of Iqbal I had just said, and realised how pertinent they were for me right now. And how ironic it was that of all the poems my new Indian Hindu housemate could have recited, that was the one he chose. A poet who was loved by both our nations.

He placed the daal down and then squeezed in between Humayun and Tariq. I still couldn't understand how they were still managing to create space.

'Say *bismillah* and begin,' Ranjit instructed us. Telling us to say the Islamic prayer said before performing any action.

How did I end up half way across the world with three crazy Pakistanis and an Indian who could recite Iqbal and told Muslims to say their prayers? As if that day couldn't have been more awkward. But that's what Britain was for us. A place where so many of us who were so different came together. It was certainly not what I was expecting. But I got used to it.

CHAPTER 5

1969

The alarm clock next to me rang ferociously, Tariq slammed his hand down and brought it to a stop. He slept on the other bad parallel to me, we shared a bedside stand between us which is where the clock was. He kept a prayer mat, hat and prayer beads in the section underneath.

I didn't sleep much, by my guess I had been up at least an hour already. I was still feeling quite anxious, on top of that I hadn't adjusted time zones yet, and it was freezing cold all night. I had lied in bed most of the night stiff trying to keep myself warm. Tariq gave out a groan.

'Salim-err...' he called out to me groggily in a typical Punjabi way.

'Yeah,' I replied.

'You up?'

'Yeah.'

Well of course I was.

'Go to the bathroom and get ready, don't take more than ten minutes or you'll make all of us late. I need to wake up Humayun.'

Humayun was snoring blissfully in his bed set horizontally at the foot of ours. There were two bedrooms in the house: me, Tariq and Humayun in this one, Ranjit and Tahir in the other.

'Takes at least ten minutes to wake the *bhanchod* up.'

I swung out of bed and opened the wooden panel painted white in front of me, inside were shelves that held all of our belongings. It acted as a wardrobe for the three of us. My trunk sat at the top, I pulled it down and took out my towel, a shirt, trousers, vest, underwear and a sweater.

'Salim?' Tariq now didn't sound so sleepy anymore. I turned to him, he was sitting up in bed. 'Don't take a shower in the mornings here you'll catch a cold'.

'Oh, OK.'

I hadn't planned on taking a shower but I realised now it wouldn't have been a bad idea. After I had devoured Ranjit's meal Tariq had shown me the room and where to put my things, and I had fallen asleep almost immediately for the first few hours before being half awake for the last few. The rest of them carried on chatting and smoking downstairs, I presumed long into the night.

'Some of us, those who had enough water, would always take a shower in the mornings in Pakistan before leaving the house. I don't know if that's the case with you. But here it's not possible, it's too cold.'

'OK, sure.'

'Take one in the evenings, there's no rush for the bathroom, and the house is warm. *Teek hain*?'

'*Teek hain*.'

'*Chalo*, head to the bathroom before someone beats you to it.'

I appreciated the advice all the guys had to give. I suppose they had all been in my situation before and probably took pity on me.

The other bedroom door was already open, I looked inside to say hello to whoever's gaze I would meet. The unmistakable tang of incense hit me. I saw Tahir performing the dawn prayer, his back towards me, I found it strange he would light incense for it. Then I looked to the left and saw Ranjit facing the wall, his eyes closed and palms together, a small statue of Ganesh sitting on a nook in front of him, two incense sticks burning either side. I was taken aback, I had only ever seen Muslim religious ceremonies, this was the first time seeing someone perform a puja, let alone seeing it being performed in the same room as a Muslim performing his prayers. I quickly hurried along unless either of them finished and saw me staring.

※ ※ ※

The sound of two quick blares of a van horn sounded from outside. It was Mawlana Ahmed, everyone scurried to finish off their breakfast and teas around the congested kitchen table. Ranjit had made paratha and masala chai, he really was as good as a cook as the rest of them had said. I put on my brown blazer, the big oversized woollen coat Mawlana had given me yesterday, and a flat cap Ranjit had given me. "Covering your head will keep you warm," he had said.

Through the front door the early brisk cold greeted us, grey clouds loomed overhead, and the smoke of hundreds of chimneys filled the sky. It was a stark contrast from the bright and colourful mornings in the village in Pakistan. As each one of us got in the van we all gave our salaams to Mawlana, who I was surprised to see was still wearing his turban and shalwaar kameez, dressed as he was the same way the day before. He returned each person's salaam and nodded his head in acknowledgement. Ranjit locked the front door behind us and was the last to get in.

'*Namaste Guru ji*,' he said with both a hint of sarcasm and sincerity as he got into the van.

All of us gave out a warm chuckle of laughter. Mawlana put on a straight face and shook his head.

'*Haraam zada*,' *Bastard*, he muttered. With that he put his foot down on the gas and the van sputtered away as Ranjit closed the doors of the van.

The streets were filled with people off to work: English, Asians, Jews, West Indians, the whole city was coming alive with a hustle and bustle. Mawlana Ahmed weaved and wound through different roads for about half an hour, until finally we reached a screeching stop. The Ford factory in Dagenham. We rolled out of the van and I looked all around me. I had never seen anything like it before, the factory sprawled out in all directions from where we were, I couldn't tell where it began and where it ended.

'Salim, come with me,' beckoned Mawlana as he came out of the front and locked the van. 'We have to sign you in. Did you bring your passport?' I took out my green Pakistani passport from my blazer. 'Good, let's go.'

We made our way across the wide car park to one side of the buildings, as the other men made their way in the opposite direction. The rumbling sounds of the factory echoed out towards us, mingling with the murmur of all the workers walking in the opposite direction to us towards the main factory entrance. Every few steps a group of Asian men would give their salaam to Mawlana which he would reciprocate, eventually it seemed like every brown person who worked here knew him.

'Morning John!' he called to one of the Englishmen. It was the first time I had heard Mawlana speak English.

'You alright mate?' came his solemn response. Even some

of the West Indians nodded their head acknowledging him as they passed.

'Mawlana what do you do at the factory?' I asked him. I was curious as everyone else was wearing work clothes: faded overalls, monotone coats, sweaters, trousers and flat caps. But Mawlana stood out in his white shalwaar kameez.

'I'm a foreman,' he replied. 'I make sure the men do their work. They realised my English was better than most of the people, even than some of the Englishmen, and because I could speak Urdu I could also talk to the Asian guys who struggled with English, so they put me in charge on one of the floors.'

'So they let you come in shalwaar kameez?'

'Oh no, I change into overalls when I start work, it's the rules. But when I'm not in the factory I wear what I want. They didn't like me even coming to work like this to begin with. But I told them look, don't worry about my clothes, trust me, I'll do more work than most of the men, and in return just let me wear my clothes outside of work. They thought I was being cocky at first but I proved them wrong!'

Typical Mawlana I thought, he was always right, even when you didn't want him to be.

We eventually reached our destination, a small brown annex building, we went in through a door that was half fake wood and half glass. The door lead to a desk with a stocky English lady sitting behind it. There were rows of women sitting behind her at their desks, drumming away at their typewriters with their fingertips.

The woman behind the desk peeked over her glasses to look at us.

'You alright Aa-med?' she asked chirpily.

'Morning Susy! You OK?'

'Yeah, fine. Who's this you got with you?'

'Ah this is my oldest friend's son from Pakistan, it's his first day at work today,' he gave a strong slap on my back lurching me forward a step.

'Oh right,' she turned towards me. 'You alright love?'

I was still struggling to understand what everyone was saying when they spoke English, and this was my first time hearing a cockney accent. I knew she had asked me a question so I just nodded my head.

'Aww he's shy,' she put on a wide smile. 'Don't worry love, you'll be fine. If you come with me, I'll get you sorted out.'

She backed her chair out and began to manoeuvre herself around her desk.

'She's going to take your details,' Mawlana began to explain in a low voice in Punjabi. 'Then they'll put you on the factory floor where they have space. They'll show you everything don't worry,' he turned back to Susy. 'OK Susy I'm off, I'll leave him in your capable hands.'

'OK dear, take care.'

'You remember where we parked?' he asked me before leaving, in his low Punjabi voice again.

'Yes.'

I couldn't remember exactly but I had an idea and knew it was in the car park somewhere.

'OK good, we'll see you at lunchtime. When we finish at 5 meet us at the van.'

'OK, thanks Mawlana.'

Mawlana turned around and went out the way we had come.

'If you come with me love.'

Susie was now standing up in front of the desk. I followed

her through a long corridor and came to a room with a man sitting at a desk writing on a piece of paper, he sat in front of a door that lead to another corridor. Across from him on the other side of the room sat three other men, two Caribbean guys and an Englishman.

'If you take a seat love, I'll put your name into the queue. Alright?'

'OK, thank you.'

I hoped I didn't sound nervous as I said it, but I probably did. I then realised that I completely understood what she had said to me. I smiled inside, I was making progress.

The rest of the day was spent having someone take my details and having safety rules explained, all the time being shifted between different rooms. Each step as boring and mundane as the last. The English had way too many rules, and way too many forms. It didn't help that I was still struggling to understand a word any of them were saying. It didn't sound anything like the English I had heard on the BBC radio service, that stuff was easy to understand. The West Indian guys would always talk to each other when there was a lull in instructions, it was the first time hearing their accent and I had even less of an idea what they were saying. How many accents did this place have?

Eventually they finally took us all out on the factory. Because I had a bit of an education behind me they put me in electrics.

'You'll start off with just putting wires in, but soon enough you'll learn how to put the whole thing together.'

This was the final desk, behind which sat a stocky man with a big bushy moustache and a receding hairline. And so my first day started off, just as he had said, plugging wires into sockets. They explained what each wire was and what all the colours meant. But essentially my first job in England, in my life, was to take coloured wires from a box as the car came down the production line and plug them all in.

At lunch I went to the canteen, I remembered my mother's advice about English food and I was a little hesitant, I didn't know if they would force me to eat pork, I thought maybe it be best just to skip lunch. No sooner had I given it a thought, that Mawlana Ahmed threw up his hand from one of the nearby tables.

'Salim-err, over here!' He was surrounded by a large group of other Asian workers, my housemates amongst them. As I approached the men immediately around him, all of whom I didn't know, made space next to Mawlana and I squeezed in.

'Here have some of my roti and keema.'

'Oh no, it's OK I'm not hungry.'

'Don't give me that just take it and eat.'

I *was* actually hungry but my attempt at being polite failed miserably.

'You didn't bring lunch with you?'

I shook my head, Mawlana looked up at Tahir and Tariq who were sitting together a short distance away from us.

'You didn't tell him to bring lunch?'

'Sorry Mawlana,' Tariq proffered. 'There were so many other things to tell him we forgot about lunch, and on top of that we were running late this morning.'

Mawlana grimaced.

'So Ranjit over there,' he pointed to Ranjit who was halfway down the table. He was midway between putting a large piece of roti and daal into his mouth, he looked up confused on hearing his name. 'Makes the dinner and the occasional breakfast for all the other lazy guys in your house. Lunch is not his responsibility as he does enough cooking as it is. The other guys either make sandwiches or try to make something that looks like roti.'

'What's a sandwich?' I asked.

'It's double-roti with cheese,' he explained.

'What's cheese'.

'*Arre yaar*, how do I explain?'

'It's like paneer,' one of the other guys explained.

'Ah yeah, call it English paneer. Has no taste, you can't cook it or it will melt with the slightest heat, typically English.'

The men around the table sniggered.

'*Bachara*,' poor guy said one of the men, 'He doesn't know what either a sandwich or cheese is!' The sniggering around the table went up a level, I felt really embarrassed.

'Leave it *yaar*,' Mawlana rebuked him. 'When you first came here you didn't know how to use a bloody toilet seat!' The sniggering turned to boisterous laughter. His sheepish expression and nod of the head admitted Mawlana had a point. Mawlana then turned to me and whispered, 'You know how to use the toilet seat right?'

'Umm, don't you just squat on top?' I whispered back.

'Oh no, don't worry I'll explain to you later.'

'How are you finding England anyway?' asked one of the other men.

'Cold,' I responded.

All the men waved their heads and murmured in agreement.

'Don't worry,' said the guy who had questioned my knowledge of cheese a moment ago. 'We all go through the same things, dealing with the cold, learning to appreciate sandwiches, using a silly toilet seat.' The men all gave out a raucous laugh. 'You'll get used to it.'

Since I had arrived in this strange place which was far away from where I grew up, both in terms of distance and culture, there was always someone there to give me a hand or offer some sincere advice. The apprehensive feeling deep down inside me started to dissipate. It was like the feeling you got the first day of school, but eventually when you made some friends and had some light-hearted conversation you knew you would get into the rhythm of things.

'Oi what's this?' a tall Englishman with blonde hair and blue overalls was standing over us. 'Eating this weird shit with your hands? You getting all that dirty sauce all over your fingers. That's fucking disgusting. You're in England now, you should be eating normal food.'

'I'm sorry if our cuisine offends you my good man.' Mawlana's responded to him instantly, his accent became more pronounced and his voice changed into something you'd hear on the English service on Radio Pakistan. "But there's plenty of other people eating their lunch with their hands. You don't eat a sandwich with a knife and fork do you? Why have you taken issue with our lunch and no one else's?'

'Of course you eat a fucking sandwich with your hands. But you're not eating sandwiches are ya?'

One of the guys at the end of the table raised the sandwich in his hand.

'Actually I am,' he said meekly.

The guys tried to muffle their laughter so as not to anger the English guy, but it was hopeless.

'David!' came a shout from the other side of the canteen, interrupting the English guy as he was about to say something. It was one of the managers with the bushy moustache I had met earlier. 'Knock it off!'

He looked down at us unsure of what to say, it seemed like

he was embarrassed, his face looked as though it was getting redder, but eventually he just walked away.

'Don't worry about these type of people Salim,' Mawlana said, as if he sensed my apprehension. 'Not all of them are like this. There are good and bad people everywhere you go.'

The men around us nodded their heads in agreement. Despite their assurances, I still felt uneasy. I looked down at the keema in my plate but I no longer felt hungry. The apprehension deep inside me came back in full force again. I was missing home.

CHAPTER 6

1969

I woke up suddenly. The alarm didn't go off. Are we late? Are we going to get sacked? I grabbed Tariq's alarm clock and looked at the time, ten past eight. I shook Tariq gently, though I really wanted to do it harder.

'Huh, huh, what is it?' he asked as he slowly came to.

'Tariq, your alarm didn't go off. We're late!'

He gave out a laugh in response.

'*Yaar*, no one told you? Saturday and Sunday is the weekend, you don't work the weekend unless they book you in for overtime.'

'Oh,' I hadn't realised, and now I felt embarrassed for having woken him. 'Right, yeah no one told me. I'm sorry.'

'It's OK *yaar*,' he still had his eyes closed. 'Go back to sleep.'

I lay back down but I was wide-awake now and didn't feel sleepy anymore. Back then in Pakistan the weekend was just Sunday, with a half-day on Friday, and it was only really a day off for school kids. People who worked just kept on working, otherwise they'd lose the opportunity to make money for the day. I guess people here could afford to take a day a few extra days off.

I lay in bed for around twenty minutes before I decided to

get up, I wasn't going to get back to sleep. I made my way downstairs to find Ranjit in the kitchen smoking a cigarette and drinking tea while reading a Hindi newspaper.

'Do you ever sleep?' I asked him.

'No, we Hindus have focused our chakras to remove the need for all worldly desires,' he used some words in traditional Hindi which we didn't have in Urdu so I was little unsure of what he said exactly so I kind of got the gist of it, but he said it with such seriousness I wasn't sure if he was joking or not. After a pause I think he realised the joke hadn't got through to me, he smiled and said 'I have insomnia.'

'Oh. Have you been to the doctor about it?'

'Yes, and an Ayurvedic pundit, but nothing. That's why I have so much time to do the cooking, which is fine because it helps me to relax. Speaking of which, do you want breakfast?'

'No, I'll just have some toast.'

I never liked toast in Pakistan, but the bread and jam here tasted way better. I would have still preferred something cooked, but Ranjit had already done so much cooking I felt awkward asking so early in the day.

'What's the plan for your first weekend?' he asked.

'I'm going to go the post office, send a letter to Ami with some money. Then I was thinking I might go explore London.'

'Ah very good, sounds like a plan. Where were you thinking of going?'

'I don't know I was just going to take the bus towards the centre of London and just walk around maybe.'

'You're going to get lost.'

'Probably, but I don't have work tomorrow so it's OK.'

We both had a chuckle.

'Just beware, if you actually want to go into a place the ticket prices are extortionate.'

'I thought as much. Besides I don't want to spend anything unless I have to in my first week.'

'Hmm,' he looked at the stairs as if to check if anyone was listening in. 'If you decide to pay to go anywhere,' he said with his voice lowered. 'Don't tell the others, they'll think you're crazy.'

'OK,' I said smiling. 'I'll try to remember.'

* * *

The number 25 bus ebbed and flowed gently as it made its way down Whitechapel Road. Another bus journey and another mindless stare out the window, this time on the other side of the world. This one was a lot smoother, most of the time, as there were fewer cracks in the road and wasn't going so fast, but as it stopped and started every few minutes it was still a bumpy bus ride.

A lady on the other side kept looking up to stare at me and I just kept staring back every time, and each time she would go back to pretending to be reading her newspaper. I had realised after a few days that people here didn't openly stare at others like they did in Pakistan, they tried to do it subtly.

I could understand why she would keep staring, if we saw someone in Pakistan who looked different to us we would probably stare at them harder than she was staring at me right now. But then there were plenty of different races and skin colours in London. I tried not to think about it and went back to looking aimlessly out the window.

Thinking about Pakistan, I remembered my bus journeys from college and how they were so different from where I was now. The wide expansive open fields were replaced with neat, albeit busy roads, the bright piercing sun was now cold and shy, stealing a peek from behind the clouds. The people going about their business all dressed and acting differently. I began to think about how many other people in the world are on a bus somewhere staring out of their window, and how different their world is right now despite the fact, they're in the same place I am.

I stayed lost in my thoughts as the bus started and stopped along its way picking up and letting go of more passengers: Old, young, talkative, silent, staring, not staring; every one of them must have had a story to tell, each one with different hopes and worries, dreams and goals. But it seemed none of them were interested in each other. Each person's story got lost every time they got off and took it with them.

Eventually as we ventured on, the Tower of London came into view. I remembered it from the journey home from the airport with Mawlana. I pulled the cord to ring the bell and made my way down the stairs. I wandered around it aimlessly just looking at it, I eventually found my way to the ticketing desk where there was an information board, and I discovered it was ordered to be built by William the Conqueror after the Battle of Hastings in 1066. None of which I really understood. Where was Hastings, was it nearby? And who was William, it sounded like an English name, so what did he conquer exactly?

I couldn't help but compare it to the Lahore Fort, which was probably made of marble and would have shone brightly in its heyday. The Tower of London looked like it was made of grey stone, and I doubted it would have been impressive at any time.

'Do you want to go inside?' asked one of the ladies in the ticketing booth. I realised I had been standing in the same spot for a while just staring up at the tower.

'Ah,' I looked up at the prices, three shillings for an adult. I had just posted most of my wages for the week to Ami. 'No it's OK, I'm just looking around.'

'Alright then,' she said with a confused expression.

I started to wander. I walked across Tower Bridge to the south side and then walked further west until I could see the bridge more clearly. Now that was something impressive to look at. Then I just kept on going along the river, until through the smog hanging over the Thames, I saw St Paul's Cathedral and then crossed over Southwark Bridge to take a look. I didn't know that it was a cathedral until I got to it, at first I thought it might be a government building of some sort. I had never been in a church, let alone a cathedral before. I wasn't sure whether they would allow non-Christians inside. When I got to the entrance I saw they also charged entry, which was strange, I could never imagine people charging to enter a mosque. I guess my lack of church attendance would have to carry on.

I traced my steps back to the Thames and this time walked along the north side. I reached the conclusion the Thames always looked muddy and brown. The sky was clear now but none of the blue in the sky reflected off the water. Black cabs and red buses continually made their way past on the roads, I took in all I had to see around me, all the people going about their weekends, families out on trips, tourists visiting the city, the hustle and bustle of the place carried on even during the weekend. I walked past the Houses of Parliament, Big Ben, Westminster Abbey, and Covent Garden Market. I didn't know the names of most of these places then, I only found out eventually what each place was over the years. I had lost track of time and I thought I may eventually get completely lost, but I didn't really care, I was too busy exploring a new world as though I was the only one in it.

By the late afternoon I reached a huge stone building with a black iron wrought fence, people were teeming around it. I eventually found a sign that read "The British Museum", another thing I would have to pay for I said to myself, as soon as the thought crossed my mind I caught the bottom of the board: "Free to the public since 1759".

I had never been inside such a large building before. The high walls and towering columns were a world away from anything I'd ever seen. I went up to a list of rooms detailing what each one contained: Ancient Egypt, Assyria, Ancient Greece, Phoenicia, Africa. The list went on and on and I hadn't even heard of half of these places. I finally found "British Isles" amidst a whole bunch of other European civilizations and wondered why they called it "The *British* Museum".

My first stop of course was the South Asia gallery. Dancing Hindu idols sat amongst calm Buddhas. I came across items from places in Pakistan like Taxila and Mohenjo-Daro that I had heard mentioned by teachers in school but never heard of anyone actually going there. It took me a journey half way across the world in a foreign place to see them. Ancient artefacts made way to relatively recent items from the Mughal period: Miniatures, pewters and weapons mostly. This stuff was more familiar to me and reminded me on the one time I went to the Lahore Museum as a child.

The South Asia and Mughal galleries lead to other parts of the Muslim world, which then lead onto other Middle Eastern civilizations I had never heard of, eventually I found a big crowd and ended up in the Ancient Egyptian gallery. The only thing I knew about the Ancient Egyptians was the story of Moses and Pharaoh, I had no idea there was so many pharaohs, which one was the one that Moses had to deal with?

'Excuse me sir,' I looked away from the plaque I was reading at the security guard next to me. 'I'm sorry but we're closing.'

I looked around it was just me and a security guard alone in the long room. The crowd that was here a few moments ago had disappeared. At least I thought it was a few moments ago.

'Oh, I'm sorry. I didn't realise.'

'It's alright sir,' he said with a warm smile. 'I'll lead you out to the exit.'

I followed him outside and was surprised to see it was dark.

'Are you alright sir?' he asked me sensing my surprise.

'Oh yes, I just didn't realise it was so late,' his already broad smile widened even further.

'It's alright sir, it's easy to get lost in the museum, in more ways than one. Happened to me many times when I first started the job. The tube station is just over to your right. Enjoy the rest of your evening.'

I thanked him and made my way out of the courtyard to the road, but I didn't go to the tube station, Mawlana had told me taking the bus was cheaper, I eventually found a route that could take me home and I watched my journey from the morning reversed, going backwards and at night. The orange streetlights glowed in the smoke of numerous chimneys, that in a way at the same time was both beautiful and ugly.

❋ ❋ ❋

When I arrived home, the air was thick with cigarette smoke, they didn't bother to open the windows because of the cold. They would rather suffocate than freeze. All of them were sitting in the kitchen having what sounded like a friendly argument, I opened the door but before I had even opened the door all the way I was greeted by Tariq standing next to it who began shouting in my direction.

'Ask Salim! See what he says.'

'What's going on?' I asked.

'Humayun wants to go to a pub.'

I was a little taken aback, that was the last thing I thought he was going to say.

'*Yaar* why are you villagers so uptight?' Humayun interjected. 'I'm from Karachi, we all drink there. Salim, you drink right? You're a young, modern guy. You study in Lahore right? After a long hard day's studying you unwind with your friends over a nice cold whiskey or something right?"

I couldn't tell if he was trying to be condescending. I just shook my head.

'*Yaar*,' Tariq began again. 'Not even Ranjit drinks and it's not even *haram* for him,' he gestured towards Ranjit calmly reading his Hindu newspaper and smoking a cigarette, pretty much in the same poise as when I had left in the morning.

'Actually in Vaishnavism it is *haram* also,' he said as he flicked to the next page.

'I don't even know what Vaishnavism is,' Tariq said confused.

'It's…never mind,' he went back to reading his paper.

'*Arre yaar*,' Humayun said to Ranjit. 'Don't tell me you haven't had a tipple, now and again.'

Ranjit smiled wryly as he took a drag from his cigarette.

'Don't involve me in an argument about alcohol with Muslims, if I get involved who knows what will happen.'

Humayun's bulging stomach made him look awkward squeezed in his chair in the tight space that was our dining area. He seemed he had become tired of arguing.

'I just want to see what it's like here. I see them from the outside and they look way better than the ones in Pakistan. We don't have to drink alcohol, they don't just sell beer'.

'Great idea,' interjected Tahir. 'Let's go to a pub to drink orange juice. Not only will we be a bunch a pakis in a pub, but we might as well be puftas as well.'

I didn't know what a pufta was, I wasn't sure if it was an

English or Punjabi word.

A silence fell over the room. Humayun slumped his head to the side in defeat, now he looked more awkward than before.

'OK, I guess I'll just have to go by myself then.'

'*Arre yaar*,' Tariq said echoing Humayun's phrase. 'I'll bloody go with you. Just take that pathetic look off your face. Who knows what these crazy Englishmen will do to you.'

'What do you mean?' I asked Tariq.

'What do you mean what do I mean?'

'Why would the English do anything to him?'

'Recently they've started not liking us Indians and Pakistanis coming here for work. A few years ago it wasn't so much of a problem. Now this National Front party has started up and they keep saying they want to send us all back.'

'It can get dangerous around here at night,' Ranjit said looking up at me from his newspaper. 'I didn't realise you would come back so late. Otherwise I would have said something when you left in the morning. All of us know someone who's been beaten up for no reason, or had a brick through the window, and a whole host of other things.'

There was a slow, sombre nod of heads around the kitchen.

'So,' Tahir turned to Humyun. 'You still want to go to the pub?'

'Yes! No one's getting killed, relax, let's just go already we talked about it long enough.'

'Fine,' Tahir seemed exasperated by now. 'I'm coming too just in case you do something stupid and Tariq needs help. Come on Salim.'

I looked at him in shock, he didn't see my expression. I

really didn't want to go with them, especially after the fact they just warned me about staying out late at night. I would have rather just stayed home and had Ranjit's food, I hadn't realised there was an aroma of gobi aloo piercing its way slowly through the cigarette smoke. He looked up at us as we all got ready to depart, but before I could say anything everyone else had put on their coats and hats, Tariq started ushering me back out of the door.

'*Chal, chal*, let's get this bloody over with.'

※ ※ ※

The smell of cigarette smoke mixed with alcohol was overwhelming. I had never smelt alcohol before, it felt like the stench was trying to reach down inside of me. The more we walked in the more stares we received, we were the only non-white people there, not surprisingly, and the place was full to the brim for the weekend. Humayun led the way through the crowd towards the bar, as each group saw us approach they would stop talking and we would be surrounded a momentary wall of silence as we walked past.

For some reason the one thing that came to my mind were the scenes in James Bond films where he would go to a high-end classy bar with beautiful women and men in fancy suits. I couldn't have been any further from that world.

Humayun saw a gap open up next to the bar and carefully moved in.

'Hello mate, you alright?' he tried asking in his best cockney accent.

The barman looked up at him with an expressionless face.

'What do you have that's not alcoholic?'

'Wa'er,' he replied plainly.

'Oh, OK. Err, four beers then please.'

'*Bhanchod*,' Tariq whispered under his breath.

'I don't want to drink beer,' I whispered to Tariq.

'Don't worry, Humayun is the only one drinking.'

Once the bartender had pulled the drunks Humayun walked back to us with all four pint glasses expertly held between his hands.

'This isn't the first time you've come to a pub have you?' Tariq asked him.

'What do you mean?'

'How are you able to hold all the glasses like that?' Tahir asked him, catching onto Tariq's line of reasoning.

'I don't know,' he stood there waiting for us to take ours from him. I didn't want it in the first place, Tariq and Tahir even less. 'Does it matter? Why does the way I hold them have anything to do with anything? Just take them already.'

We all looked at each other.

'We'll hold them for you while you have your first.'

Tariq handed us a pint each and left one for Humayun. A smile crept onto his face.

'Now that you have it, why not just try it?'

I took a sniff.

'It stinks.'

'It doesn't taste as bad as it smells.'

Without thinking about it much I took a sip off the head. Tariq subtly raised his eyebrow at me and Humayun smile widened and his cheeks became puffier than seemed possible.

'It tastes as bad, or maybe even worse than it smells.'

Humayun's smile faded and now one crept onto both Tariq and Tahir's faces.

'Hurry up and finish your first one,' Tahir said to him. 'Then we can all get rid of ours, the smell is killing me.'

'Why did you have to drag us out with you?' Tariq asked him. 'You could have just come by yourself and not told us.'

'*Yaar*, I don't like the way they stare at me,' he realised he couldn't carry on with the façade any longer. 'I used to come with Junaid before he moved to Manchester.'

'Why am I not surprised, that guy was as stupid as you are.' He turned to me. 'He was the one living with us before you came here.'

'Come on *yaar*, don't be like that,' Humayun pleaded. 'We live in this country now, we have to try to fit in.'

Tariq's expression changed abruptly. Before he was mildly annoyed, now he was angry.

'You try fitting in!' Tariq's voice was louder, and more people in the pub were looking at us. 'I'm Pakistani, and I always will be, you want to pretend to be a white man, go ahead, but don't drag us along with you!'

I was glad on the one hand he was talking in Urdu so everyone else didn't hear his white man remark, but on the other hand everyone was staring at him talking angrily in a foreign language.

Tariq handed his beer to Humayun, then grabbed mine and placed it between Humayun's arm and torso, so he was left standing with our three drinks awkwardly, the froth from all three spilling onto his jacket. Tahir put his one down on a table on the side.

'Come on, let's leave *gora sahib* to enjoy his drinks,' Tariq said.

He stormed off away from us and out the door, a gaze of white faces watching him leave just as inquisitively as they had watched us come in. I looked at Humayun with his helpless expression. I felt sorry for him, but I didn't want to be here with all these people staring at us, I felt more a foreigner in this one place than I had done the entire week.

'Sorry *yaar*,' I left him there and imagined he looked on at me with the same expression, unsure of what to do next.

Tariq was standing outside looking at the sky, the murmur of the pub now behind us as we faced the silence of the night.

'If you want to stay with *gora sahib* you can,' he said while he carried on looking at the sky. 'But he can't even find his backside on a good day, so who knows if he can find his way home drunk.'

'Let's just go home,' Tahir offered.

I nodded my head in agreement as we started to make our way back.

'Why did you get so angry with him all of a sudden?' I asked Tariq after we had walked a few steps.

'I don't know. I'm just sick and tired of us demeaning ourselves to be here.'

'What do you mean?'

The air was cold and sharp, the smell of burning coal was heavy in the air and all the chimneys were unfurling their sails of smoke, but there was hardly any wind to billow them. The sound of the voices of the pub slowly faded into the distance and all we could hear were our shoes scraping and echoing off the pavement slabs. I looked at him as he thought. The yellow street lights made it hard to see his features but I could tell he was thinking.

'Would you believe me if I told you I was a history

teacher?'

I tried to look at him through the yellow glow again. He must have been between 30 and 35, in the week I had been here he had always had a light and candid mood. But as I looked at him and the features of his face, he carried with him the signs of someone who knew much more than their years could tell them. Someone who could carry authority and purpose with their actions, just like a teacher. This whole time I was thinking Ranjit was the educated one, the other two had made it seem that way at least.

'Yeah, I could believe that,' I told him.

His wide smile stretched out his moustache.

'I left working as a teacher to work in a factory. Can you imagine? There was a time people would look up to and respect teachers. Now we go off to work in the English factories because they pay more.'

'I was going to do English Literature at university.' After I said it, I wasn't sure I felt the need to mention it.

'Hmm, yeah you look the type. A kindred spirit. An intellectual who no one would pay for.'

We both chuckled.

'You never told me you were a teacher,' Tahir said to him. 'So this whole time, I've been the only dumb one in the house?'

'No that's not true,' Tariq said. 'Humayun is the dumb one.'

'I still don't understand why you got so angry with him,' I said.

'Studying history gives you perspective Salim. When you've read about all the things the English did in India, from the East India Company to Jallianwala Bagh, to the mess they left after partition. After all that, and the independence we fought for, that our people died for, we still ended up coming here to work for them. It's ironic don't you think?'

'We're not going to stay here forever. No one is. Everyone will go back eventually.'

He stopped, turned and looked at me.

'Have you ever heard of anyone going back to Pakistan? I certainly haven't. Ask Ranjit about his Indian friends, they're the same.'

'We haven't been here for very long. Eventually most of us will go back, and then some other guys will come along to work.'

'Hmm,' he turned around and started walking again. 'We'll see.'

'So you're angry at Humayun because he wants to go to a pub and drink alcohol and be like a white man?'

'If he wanted to go to a pub and drink and do whatever he wanted that's his business. But then we he drags us into it and then justifies it by saying we need to fit in, well, that's where I draw a line. I'm not interested in "fitting in". Why should we? If we're so desperate to fit in why did so many people have to die so we could be independent? Why didn't we just let the British keep ruling over us?'

I didn't know what to say. I hadn't really thought about any of this. I remembered back to when Imran was so desperate to come here to earn a living. It was just so common and so easy to think that coming here to work was the thing to do, but no one ever thought about it, not the way Tariq did at least.

We walked the rest of the way home in silence. Ranjit was still in the kitchen when we arrived, smoking his cigarette and reading his newspaper, as if we had never left.

'That was quick. Where's Humayun?'

'Don't ask,' was Tahir's sole response.

'*Teek*,' He looked up at me, I simply made a face as if to say, "yeah, don't ask". 'Do you have space for aloo gobi?' he asked us.

Tariq was already taking the plates and the hot pot with the rotis out. We ate in silence and said nothing for the rest of the evening. By the time we had all gone to bed and fallen asleep Humayun still wasn't home, and I no longer cared.

CHAPTER 7

Present

I made my way down out of the attic. If I didn't leave now I'd never get out. Linda was at the kitchen sink doing the dishes, she didn't hear me walk up behind her, I held the photo of us in a bar in Soho in front of her.

'Oh my God,' she turned the tap off and took of her gloves to hold the photo and look at it closer. 'Look at us, so young and naive. That was our first date.'

'And our most awkward,' I added.

'First dates are always awkward.'

'I wouldn't know, I only ever had one.' She looked up at me with her wide brimmed smile, the one I used to see a lot more of when we were younger, but it became less frequent now.

'What I wouldn't give to go back to those days.'

'What would you have done differently?'

'Well, I would have certainly bought you a new suit.'

'I'll never hear the end of my suit.'

She gave out a nasal laugh. Another thing she used to do when we were younger. It was like all my memories had decided to come back to me today.

'What would you have done differently? Knowing what you know about us now?'

'Nothing, I loved every moment we spent together.'

She wrapped her arms around me and kissed me on the cheek. A rare moment of intimacy between us now in our age. As she held me there, I began to think, would I have done something differently? Marrying Linda was one of the hardest things I went through in my life. She was the reason I stopped talking to Ami, the reason why I now regretted being away from her for so long. Had I done something differently knowing what I know now? Would I have even married Linda? A feeling of despair washed over me as to why I even asked the question to myself. As if she could feel what I was thinking, she let go of our embrace and looked me in the eyes.

'What's wrong Salim?'

I looked up into her eyes. I didn't have an answer.

CHAPTER 8

1969

'Come on mate, it's lunchtime!'

I looked out from underneath the steering column to see Matt staring expectedly.

'Sorry mate,' I replied, the word was new to me and I still felt awkward saying it. 'I'm almost done.'

I finished tightening the screw on the end of the wire I was putting in and crawled my way out. I hadn't realised the whistle had sounded, or that the conveyor of Cortinas making their way through the factory had even stopped moving. Most of the other workers in our part of the factory had already left.

'You alright mate? You seem a bit distant.'

Matt and I had started on the same day. He was the only English guy in my first week I talked to regularly. We worked together on getting the car's wiring in place before it got to the next stage of the production line.

'Yeah I'm alright. Just tired is all.'

'You didn't get smashed on your first week's pay did ya?'

He put on his wide toothy smile. He was skinny with ginger hair and had one of his front teeth missing. It all added up to a gawky look when he smiled. I forced myself to smile back, I didn't know what "getting smashed" meant. I didn't know a lot of the things Matt talked about.

'No mate. Just, you know. Two days off and then you're back again.'

I didn't mention the long journey all the way to the British Museum, or the adventure to the pub.

'Why you don't have weekends in India?'

'Pakistan. Yeah, we do, but this is my first job out of school.'

'Yeah I know what you mean mate. No more paper rounds or chasing girls at the youth club no more.'

He managed to make his toothy grin wider and I still had no idea what he was talking about. What was a paper round? And I thought youth clubs were for just playing snooker. Not that I had ever been to a youth club.

'Don't worry you'll get used to it.'

He elbowed me gently as we made our way out of the factory floor, I stopped to get my lunchbox out of the locker and we made our way towards the cafeteria.

Coming back to work from the weekend wasn't the issue. At least at work I was keeping busy. The truth was I was still a little upset about our misadventure at the pub, I had thought about the fact that all my housemates had stories of friends being harassed. What if that had happened to us? What would Ami have thought about me getting hurt in my first week? I tried to tell myself I was exaggerating but I couldn't get the thoughts out of my head.

As we reached the cafeteria, Matt made his way to the line for the canteen food as I made my way over to the usual table of Asians.

'I'll see you back at the floor yeah?' He knew the answer

already but he would always ask it anyway.

'Yes mate.'

The Asians, as usual, were laughing and joking amongst themselves, making the most of their break to unwind and relax. If it weren't for their overalls and surroundings you'd have thought they were still in India or Pakistan, bobbing their heads and twisting their hands the way that they do when they talk.

'Make space for Salim,' Anwar instructed the line of guys with their backs towards me as I approached the table.

Tariq and Humayun were on opposite sides. Humayun had kept his glum embarrassed face all weekend, he still had it now. Before I had even sat down the guy on my right, whose name I couldn't remember, and who looked freakishly similar to Munny turned to me.

'I heard you had a right proper *piss up* at the local.'

The table erupted in laughter except for Humayun.

'What? No!' I shook my head vigorously. 'We went in, we left. We didn't drink anything. Honest!'

'We know *yaar*, we know,' Anwar tried to reassure me. 'Tariq told us, Waqas is just pulling your leg.'

I looked at him to see his smile taking up most of his face. He had succeeded in embarrassing me with hardly any effort. I thought they would have looked down on me if they had thought we had gone drinking. Or that I had even had a sip.

'Nothing wrong with a little *tipple* now and again,' said Gurminder, one of Sikh guys. He wore a large dark blue turban to match his overalls. 'Though beer is disgusting. I much prefer whiskey.'

'*Yaar*, don't talk like that, if Mawlana Ahmed heard you he'd give you a right earful,' Tariq warned him jokingly. 'And don't give the kid any ideas.'

'Where is Mawlana today?' I asked.

'He's so embarrassed that you went to a pub he didn't want to see you today,' said one of the guys a few seats down.

If the table hadn't laughed at the statement I would have thought it was true.

'He's working a double shift,' Anwar reassured me again. 'He likes to skip lunch so he can finish early.'

'That man is not human, he's more like one of King Solomon's jinns,' said one of the other guys. 'Fasting every Monday and Thursday, keeping his *wuzu* for the whole shift and sneaking prayers in on the line while nobody notices.'

The men at the table nodded their head in agreement, even the non-Muslim ones. But this time no one laughed at the statement, despite the fact it sounded like it was meant to be a joke.

'Why were you late for lunch today?' asked Anwar.

'Oh, I just got stuck doing something, I wanted to finish it before I came here.'

Anwar didn't seem convinced, he looked at me questioningly.

'You're homesick. I can tell, it's your first week. Eventually you'll get used to it, and all the stupid things these idiots get up to,' he motioned towards the men sitting round the long canteen table. 'It's normal, you'll get over it.'

I nodded my head, maybe all these random scenarios in my head were just a result of me being homesick. I thought I was over it, but I had only been here a week, I still had a lot to learn, still had a lot to get used to. Tariq looked around the table.

'*Chiliye?*' Shall we go?

'*Chalo,*' let's go, they echoed together in response.

'We'll see you tomorrow, *inshallah*.'

'*Inshallah*.'

As the group made their way back to the factory floor I started thinking about home. I was wondering how Ami and Abbas were a week after I had left. Was Abbas still upset? Was Ami worried? Who was Imran hanging out with now? I hadn't really been thinking about them much and I started to feel guilty about it. I was looking forward to getting a response to my letter, I didn't know how long it would take mine to get there, and then how long it would take for them to send me one back.

'Excuse me?'

I looked up to see who had broken up my train of thought. She had brown hair and green eyes, I had never seen that combination before, a shy smile across her face. I was slightly taken aback, I had hardly talked to any women since I arrived here, I thought maybe she was waiting to grab a table for a group of her female colleagues and wanted me to get up.

'Yes?'

'Were you at the Duke of Wellington on Saturday?'

'The what?'

'The Duke of Wellington, it's a pub in Whitechapel.'

'Err, yes,' I responded slightly unsure, I didn't know what the name of the pub was but I assume it must have been that one. 'How did you know?'

'I was there too, I saw you just now and thought you looked familiar. I just wanted to ask, what happened that night? The man you were with seemed really angry with your friend. We were all talking about it afterwards and thinking about what must have made him so upset.'

'Oh, he just, well, you see. None of us drink, well, only one of us did, and the rest of us didn't want to, but he kind of wanted us to.'

I felt really embarrassed that I couldn't say a complete sentence without making any mistakes.

'Oh,' she seemed a little surprised at the banality of what happened. 'Then why did you go to the pub in the first place?'

'I, don't actually know, and have been wondering the same thing.'

She giggled, at first I thought she may have done it to sound polite, but it didn't come across that way, it made the hair of the back of my neck stand on end. I had never had a casual conversation with a girl before. She placed her tray on the table and sat down across from me.

'Do you mind if I join you?'

'No, of course not.'

'I'm Linda.'

'Salim.'

'That's a nice name.'

I smiled, I didn't know what to say to that.

'Where are you from Salim?'

She placed her fork into her food, and started to break apart the mash potato she had.

'Pakistan.'

'Whereabouts?' I was started to think maybe she was trying to be condescending, from what I had gathered English people didn't really like Asians very much, and they hardly socialised.

'A little place outside of a city called Lahore.'

'Oh yeah,' she looked up and squinted her eyes thinking. 'That's in the Punjab right? North West of India?'

I was taken aback, all the English people I met knew nothing about things outside of England.

'How do you know that?'

'My dad was born in Calcutta.'

'Really?'

'Yeah,' her smile widened. 'My grandfather was an officer during the Raj. He would *always* go on about India. Well you know, it was all India back then, I'm sure you know.'

She picked up the pepper on the table and sprinkled it lightly on the mash.

'Yeah,' I was feeling a little unsure about myself, but the more she spoke the more I realised she was being genuine and I slowly started to relax the more we talked.

'Your father's in the army too?'

'Oh no! My grandad and my dad didn't exactly have the best of relationships. But I got on fine with both of them. I spent a lot of time with my grandad, going through his old scrapbooks, and looking at maps. That's why I knew that you were from the Punjab.' She giggled again, some people might have found it incessant and annoying, I didn't. 'But yeah, my dad would never have wanted to join the army. My grandad was a bit of a brute, and, if I'm going to be honest, a bit of an alcoholic, spent most of the family money drinking and gambling.' She stopped and shook her head. 'Sorry I'm rambling.'

'It's OK. This is a lot more interesting than my usual lunch breaks.'

She laughed, and all of a sudden I felt lighter.

'So how long have you been in England?'

'A week.'

'Really? Your English is very good. There's loads of guys

who have been here years and still can't put a sentence together.'

Ironic, given my first sentence came out that way.

'I studied English at college.'

'Ah I went to college too, there's not much going for an East End girl with an education though so that's why I ended up here. How come you're here?'

'They pay more here.'

'Oh OK.'

There was an awkward silence, I didn't know what to say. I just watched her eating her lunch, and for some reason it was enjoyable.

'So,' she didn't look up from her food. 'Are you going to eat your lunch or are you just going to watch me eat mine?'

'Oh, err, yeah I, yeah I am.'

I took a bite from my sandwich and chewed it on hastily.

'How come I never see other women here at lunchtime?' I asked her with my mouth full.

'Oh, most of the girls prefer to come a little later when all the men head back. You know it's a little weird having all of them here staring at you when you just want to have lunch. I was just too hungry to wait today'.

I nodded my head.

'Which part of the floor do you work on?'

'Electrical.'

'One of the smart ones, I should have known. How are you finding it?'

'It's good. I like it.'

She nodded her head, it felt as though she never got rid of her smile.

'Where do you work?'

'Clerical.'

'What do they do there?'

'Like secretary work. Lots of typing, filling out forms. It's alright, pays the bills. But I wouldn't want to do it for the rest of my life.'

'What would you rather be doing?'

'Oh, I don't know,' her smile turned to a mischievous one and she shook her hair gaily. 'World famous ballet dancer, Hollywood actress, whatever!'

'I can see you as an actress.'

She lowered her head, her awkward smile became a shy one.

'Whatever, no one likes a tease.'

'I mean it.'

'Yeah well, there's only so much you can dream of doing if you're from the East End, even if you have been to college.' She looked pensively at her watch. 'I have to head back, I only had time for a quick lunch today. It was really nice meeting you, and I'm sorry if I was being nosy before.'

'Oh no, it was fine.'

'I guess I'll see you around?'

'Sure.'

She got up and turned her back and started to walk away, I wanted to say something, I didn't want her to go, I couldn't find the words to do it, but then she stopped as though she had heard my thoughts and turned back.

'So, err, the Duke may not be up your street, it's not really mine, you don't really get much a of a choice around this part of town. Anyway, I know this really swell place in Soho that you might like to go to sometime? You know if you wanted to, like see a much more, *cosmopolitan* side of London.'

'I don't know what that word means.'

She gave out a nasal laugh.

'But yeah why not?'

'Great, well shall we meet outside the Duke at 7 on Friday and we can make our way from there?'

'Sounds like a plan.'

'Swell, I guess I'll see you then.'

I nodded my head.

'Great, see ya.'

She walked away and I just sat there watching her leave. What just happened? Did she ask me out on a date? It felt surreal, I wasn't sure if I was dreaming, my insides felt like they had filled up with air. Before she left the cafeteria she turned back and saw me staring at her, she waved as she went through the door. I waved back numb, not sure what to do.

'Ah mate she's a stunner!'

Matt seemingly appeared out of nowhere, but of course I knew he was in the cafeteria the same time as me.

'Did you pull?'

He elbowed me in the ribs like he always did when he put on his toothy grin.

'Did I what?'

'Did you ask her out?'

'Erm, yeah. Well, I think she asked *me* out.'

Matt raised his eyebrows and widened his eyes.

'What? You just met her and like that and she asks you

out like that?'

I nodded my head, slightly unsure.

'Well, she just asked me if I'd like to go out with her. Does that mean she asked me out?'

'Yes mate! That's what asking out means. She sounds like a keeper! Come on mate let's get back to it. You, and me, can daydream about her later.'

I hastily cleared my rubbish into my metal lunchbox and walked back with him to the floor. My mind was all over the place.

* * *

I stood a distance away from the Duke of Wellington around a corner from the entrance where the street lighting didn't reach, so no one could see me standing there. The raucous laughter inside spilled out onto the street a little more each time someone opened the door to go in or out. The clinking of glasses, the cacophony of chatter, it all put me on edge for some reason. Maybe because the idea of going out for a drink was still so alien to me, coming from somewhere where drinking was done in secret and severely frowned upon if it ever came out into the open. Here it was just a part of life. Add to that the stories I kept hearing from different guys at the factory of run ins they had with drunk people, plus the awkwardness of going inside the actual place the last weekend with Humayun and Tariq meant I felt a lot better just waiting in the shadows.

I looked at my watch again for what felt like the tenth time, I was still early. I had started using a flat cap to keep warm, but I didn't wear it this evening as I thought it would ruin my hair. God, just the thought of me getting riled about getting my hair ruined made me despise myself. What had I become? What has this girl done to me? I had used Brylcreem for the first time, and I couldn't stop touching my hair afraid the wind had unsettled it. I kept thinking about Imran and how not so long ago I had made fun of him being so fussy with his hair. Now here I was getting the top of my ears frozen off.

I heard the sound of a solitary pair of heels clicking against the pavement coming closer. I peered around the corner to have a look but didn't want to give myself away in case it wasn't her. She stopped in front of the pub where it illuminated a spot on the street. It was her, she wore a yellow sweater with a miniskirt and tights, she had put makeup on and even in the dim light I could see it accentuated her green eyes.

I stepped out of the darkness and she was startled for a moment.

'Where did you come from?'

'I was waiting here like we agreed, erm, shouldn't I have been?'

'Well yeah, but you didn't have to pop out of the dark and scare me like that.'

We both gave out a shy laugh.

'You alright?' she asked.

'Yeah,' our breath entwined in the cold air. 'You?'

'Yeah I'm alright, bit cold but that's how it always is. You ready?'

'Yeah.'

She looked at me with her smile as we began to walk. I took a moment to think about what to say, I needed to say something.

'You look really nice,' I finally managed.

'Thanks, you don't look too bad yourself. Though, I'm not so sure about that suit.'

My heart sunk. I was wearing the brown wool suit Ami had given me.

'What's wrong with it? My mum gave it to me.'

'Yeah it looks it too.'

We walked for a while in silence until we reached Whitechapel station, bought our tickets to Leicester Square and sat down on the westbound District Line train. I was trying to not to think about what she said about my suit. The train travelled raggedly moving side to side as it made its way through the different stations. I think we could both tell we were both trying to think of something to say.

The stares from strangers continued as normal, I had learned to just ignore them, but I couldn't tell if there was a sense of indignance this time because Linda and I were together. I thought maybe the men were just looking at her because she was pretty, a part of me wanted to protect her from those gazes, but the few children and elderly women who were on the train this late were also staring.

'I'm sorry about what I said about your suit,' she said breaking my train of thought. 'It's very nice.'

'No it's not.'

She gave out that nasal laugh of hers.

'It's the best I could get where I came from.'

'Maybe we can go shopping next time.'

'I don't know if I can afford a new suit right about now.'

'Well let me know when you get a raise and we'll go out.'

'Are we going out?'

'What do you mean?'

'I mean, is this a date?'

'Do you want it to be?'

'I don't know, do I have to do anything?'

She let out a cackle.

'You've never been on a date before have you?'

I shook my head.

'It's just in Pakistan you don't really go out with girls who you're not related to.'

'So, you go out on dates with, like your sister?' she looked at me incredulously.

'No! I mean...'

She couldn't keep her straight face and burst out into laughter.

'I know what you mean. I'm just making fun of you. Remember I told you my granddad always talks about India? He would also talk about the things people do differently over there, like how parents choose who their kids marry, that they never take baths but always showers,' she lowered her voice. 'And that they don't use toilet paper.'

We both laughed.

'Why did your granddad even bother to mention that?'

She shook her head slowly.

'He's starting to lose his marbles in his old age,' her voice became quieter and her smile faded. 'He starts talking about all these strange things he never used to, or shouldn't really talk about, he just ends up muttering to himself and talking nonsense sometimes.'

She looked down at her feet and the whole carriage strangely fell silent, as though everyone felt the solemnness of the moment. The only noise was the sound of the train as it carried on its journey through London, the electric lights through the windows reflected on Linda's face as they changed shape then faded, then came back again.

'Anyway, it doesn't matter, I'm sure he'll get better soon,' she said quickly. Her smile slowly started to come back and she looked at me. 'So you've...never been with someone before.'

'What do you mean?'

'You know, like held hands or kissed, or...anything?'

'No.'

I was trying not to feel embarrassed, I was afraid she was starting to think less of me. She reached over and gently grabbed my hand, that single touch felt like euphoria, my skin tingled, her hand was cool and soft.

'It's OK,' she looked straight at me with a reassuring glance. 'You don't have to feel embarrassed.'

She was perfect, I never wanted to leave this moment. I wanted to ask her to marry me there and then, like a scene out of some corny Indian movie, but common sense held me back. I didn't realise fate would eventually take care of the rest for me.

We changed for the Northern Line at Embankment and took it two stops to Leicester Square. The whole place was alive with people and bright lights, music streamed out of numerous bars and clubs. It seemed like a world far removed from the Duke of Wellington, even though it was only a few tube stops away.

Linda led me by the hand through the small busy roads through crowds of young people, some of them going from one venue to another, some of them just standing around smoking and drinking, it seemed like every other building had something going on. No one seemed to be staring at us here, everyone just went about doing their own thing.

'Here we are.'

I looked up at the building in front of us, "The Marquee Club".

'What's so special about this place?'

'You'll see,' she put on a wry smile. 'You into Rock and Roll?'

'I don't know, let's find out.'

She gave out a short laugh as we went in. The place was heaving with people centred around the stage at the front where a band was playing out a lively song. I had never heard anything like it before. There were four of them dressed in skinny black suits with white shirts and black ties. The frontman was giving all he had, I couldn't understand how he was able to sing and play his guitar together so vivaciously. The drummer behind him was just as fast and his beat was mesmerising, the crowd in front of them were bobbing their heads to the beat.

'Do you want a drink?'

We had arrived at the bar, the whole time I was looking at the band as she was dragging me through the crowd.

'I don't drink.'

'Do you want a coke at least?'

'OK sure.'

As she turned away to wait her turn at the bar I scanned around taking it all in. Another new experience for me that felt totally out of this world. But this didn't make me feel awkward or out of place for some reason. Maybe it was Linda, maybe it was the music. Or maybe it was being in a place full of white faces and none of them looking at me.

'Hey Linda!' a voice shouted from behind me.

It was a black guy, he was muscular and easily the tallest one in the building. He was wearing a blue dinner jacket.

'Hey Dan! You alright?'

The embraced and I felt awkward. Linda turned to me.

'This is Salim.'

Dan held out his hand.

'What's going on brother?'

'Hello', I didn't know what else to say I just took his hand and smiled. He had a firm grip but his palm was smooth.

'Dan works at the factory with us.'

'Ah you're at Ford too,' said Dan. 'Are you on the assembly line?'

'Yeah, in electrical.'

'Ah that's why I haven't seen you,' he had a wide smile with immaculate teeth. 'I'm about a mile before you in the body frame section.'

'Oh right, swell.'

I hoped I had used the word correctly.

Dan turned to Linda.

'There's a group of us over in the booths if you guys want to join us later.'

'Alright, maybe in a bit yeah?'

'Nice one,' he turned back to me. 'Nice meeting you brother enjoy your evening.'

He gave a gentle slap on the arm and made his way back the way he came, his body swaying to the music as he walked.

'We went out for a bit.'

That came as a surprise.

'He's a nice guy, but, he was a bit too wild for me.'

I was taken aback.

'What do you mean?'

She rolled her eyes.

'He was always wanting to go out, and party and be doing something. When sometimes I'd just be like, you know what? I want to stay home and put my feet up. Honestly I don't know how he affords to go out so much.'

I felt calmer now knowing what she meant, though I don't know why I had this sudden pang of jealousy.

'But don't get me wrong, he's a really nice guy. He actually has a Jamaican accent, he just covers it with a cockney one to fit in better. If you spend enough time with him he'll forget and he'll switch between the two, it's hilarious.'

'Can I ask you a personal question?'

'Course'.

'How come you don't go out with English guys?'

Her smile became mischievous in a way I could tell she was about to tease me.

'Who says I don't?'

'Sorry, I just assumed you didn't'.

She gave out a nasal laugh and held my hand, the touch of her skin made my arm feel like it was tingling.

'I go out with whoever I want. Is that alright with you?'

'As long as you're only going out with me right now.'

She pulled me forward and kissed me.

'You better make a good impression then.'

She turned around to pick up our drinks and left me with my head spinning. What just happened?

The rest of the night we talked, jumped up and down to the different bands that played, we hung out with Dan and his friends; he was going out with a woman from Barbados, and she had an Irish friend who was going out with an English guy, I couldn't remember their names just their nationalities for some reason. We did so much but it seemed like it went by so quickly. We stayed the whole night, and only left when the final band had slowly started to wind down.

The tube was shut so we walked to Oxford Circus to take the 25 bus. Once we got out of Soho the streets were empty, the quietness pierced by Linda's talking. She sounded more excited and happier, the alcohol had loosened her up, not that she was holding anything back before, but now she was slightly louder and had more things to say. I didn't care, I forgot almost everything we talked about, mundane things like food and films, I just wanted to spend all my time with her.

'You haven't said anything for a while.'

We were the only two on the top deck of the bus, I was staring out into the abyss as usual on one side, and her voice was gently soothing me on the other but then she forced me out of my pseudo-slumber.

'I was just listening.'

'Oh really, what was I talking about then?'

'You were talking about how your mum did so well raising you and your brother while working at the same time, so don't understand why she's so keen for you to settle down and become a full-time mum. You think it might be because she feels like her mum did a better job of raising her and her siblings, but you think your mum did a fantastic job regardless. And anyway, you're not too keen on settling down just yet anyway. Your mum's a bit old-fashioned and doesn't realise that things aren't how they used to be –'

'OK OK, so you were listening I get it. I'm sorry I ever doubted you.'

'You didn't just doubt me, you also doubted my skill to daydream and listen attentively at the same time.'

'A very important life skill I'm sure. So what's your mum

like?'

The question threw me a bit, I didn't expect her to ask me that.

'She's nice, but she has a tough time looking after the land we own. My dad died when my brother and I were young, so she kind of fell into running his day to day business: Keeping a check on farmers, making sure they pay their rent, making sure things are still growing in the fields. Not a lot of women in Pakistan do the kinds of things she does.'

'I like her already. Going against the grain, not letting other people's expectations define her.'

'Yeah I suppose you could say that, never really thought about it that way. I always just felt she was burdened with something that she didn't want. But then it has made her stronger, more confident. I don't think she would be who she is if it weren't for her circumstances.'

The bus roared and churned its way on. With few people getting on and off and no traffic it moved faster and more ferociously than during the day.

'Do you think I would ever meet her?'

I had never seen a white person in Pakistan, not even in Lahore. I couldn't imagine this young, pretty white girl coming to the village, having to explain who she was and how I knew her, why she was travelling with me, having to learn how to eat roti and salan, having to use a squat toilet, it was completely unimaginable.

'I don't know If you would like Pakistan. It's very different to here.'

'You came from there to here and seem to be doing fine.'

'Oh I've had my fair share of issues.'

'So it's not like some exotic place where you can just escape to and ride elephants through the jungle.'

I gave out a chuckle.

'No I'm afraid not. You could go to the Shalimar Gardens and pretend you're a Mughal princess for a while, but that's about it.'

She kissed me and I kissed her back, we held each other in our embrace for a long time until eventually she stopped and rested her head on my shoulder.

'What was that for?'

'I just felt like it.'

We stayed like that for the rest of the way home. I guess she was tired and no longer wanted to say or hear anything more. We walked to the Duke of Wellington pub where we had started the night and that's where we finished it before we parted ways with a final kiss. Just like a dream it had finished before I had even realised it had started.

CHAPTER 9

Present

As the phone started to ring with the international tone I became pensive. It felt strange having this feeling calling my own brother.

'*Alo?*'

The voice didn't sound familiar, but I hadn't spoken to him in around twenty years I wasn't sure what he sounded like anymore.

'*Alo?*' he repeated.

'Abbas?'

He didn't respond.

'Salim?' he asked eventually, a part of me was glad he recognised my voice.

'Yes, it's me. How are you?'

'Fine, *alhumdulilah.*'

'Good, good,' This was going to be harder than I thought. 'I got your letter, about Ami. I wished you had told me sooner, I would have-'

'I didn't send you a letter.'

'What?'

'I said I didn't send you a letter.'

My insides turned.

'I got a letter yesterday telling me Ami had died.'

'She died two days ago, the funeral was yesterday. I, don't know...even if I had sent it, I don't know how you would have got it so soon.'

'What...' my mind was running circles, how could this have been possible? Who could have sent it? Was this some sick joke? It came in the normal post how could it have arrived so early?

'Salim, maybe Ami sent it.'

'Did she know she was going to die?'

'She never said anything to me, she hadn't been to see the doctor as far as I know. It happened suddenly, she was taking a nap in the afternoon. We went to wake her up for prayer but, she didn't...Maybe she just knew.'

As crazy as it sounded, and as much as I wanted to dismiss it, it was the only explanation that made sense.

'I'm sorry I didn't call you sooner, I was looking everywhere for your number. But I couldn't find it amongst Ami's things.'

'It's fine,' there was a silence between us, neither of us knew what we wanted to say.

'How is your family?' he asked eventually.

'Fine, *alhumdulilah*. How is yours?' I tried to think of their faces in the photos Ami had sent years ago. 'Are you a grandfather yet?'

He laughed softly.

'Yes, I have four grandchildren now. You?'

'My first is on its way.'

'Just one so far? Salim you're the older one!'

'Children come slowly in England.'

He laughed again, it had a tinge of the way he used to laugh when he was young. I stopped feeling pensive and felt glad we were both relaxed.

'Salim, do you ever think about coming back?'

'My home is here now.'

'I know that, I mean to visit. There will always be a place for you here if you want it. Don't you want to see your old home again, see me, your family, walk down the roads you grew up on. I remember when we were young you used to say how you loved the smell of grass when it rained, don't you ever miss that?'

I had forgotten I had ever said that, but now I remembered, and the earthy smell of fresh rain filled my nostrils. I remembered the last time I visited the village when it rained was in the 70s after I proposed to Linda. My memories started running through my mind again, I began to remember our house and where we used to play as children, where Abbas's grandchildren now most likely played, I could hear the thunder in the distance and the rain pouring down onto the roof, as if my memories and my thoughts began to play and intermingle with each other.

'Why don't you come back?' he asked me again. 'Who knows how long it will be before one of us follows Ami. You should come back at least once before then.'

'Ever since I got the letter it's all I've been thinking about, my life here, and the mistakes I made.'

'Our life runs how God wants it to, our mistakes are there so we learn from them, not mourn for them.'

I had been contemplating and thinking over it for the last

few days, and now Abbas had helped me make up my mind.

'You're right, it's time I came home.'

CHAPTER 10

1971

'Today in East Pakistan bloodshed and violence continued to rage on the streets of numerous cities, including Dhaka and Chittagong as West Pakistan continues Operation Searchlight.'

All of us in the house were glued to the small black and white tv we had rented together and put into the corner of the dining area. Images of tanks rolling over roads, people fleeing and soldiers firing into the air flickered on the screen in grey imagery. Ranjit was cooking in the kitchen but he was listening. The room was silent as the aroma of cooking and cigarette smoke wafted around the room.

'*Yaar* what has gotten into Yahya's mind.'

Tariq was talking about General Yahya Khan, the president of Pakistan who had ordered the West Pakistani forces to invade after East Pakistan, now Bangladesh, declared independence from West Pakistan.

'He's reining the bastards in is what he's doing,' was a typical response from Humayun.

'Reining them in?' Have you been drinking again? We're massacring our own people because they won an election.'

Humayun just shook his head, he had no response, he was wrong about a lot of things a lot of the time, and he was too lazy to have a response.

'Ranjit,' Tariq turned to him. 'Tell your boys not to get involved. We don't want to embarrass them.'

'Yeah because your boys did so well last time.'

'We'll call that one a draw.'

They were talking the war between Pakistan and India in 1965.

'Call it what you want. But what's happening in Bangladesh is a genocide. This isn't going to end well for Pakistan.'

Humayun turned his head to say something, but gave up, he knew his nationalist pride wasn't going to win any arguments.

The phone rang but no one moved to answer it.

'I'm kneading dough someone get it,' Ranjit called out.

'Salim,' Tariq broke my concentration from the news. 'Pick up the phone, it's probably Linda anyway.'

'Oh right, yeah.'

She said she was going to call. I went to the hallway and picked up the receiver.

'Hello?'

'Hey handsome.'

I put on my heaviest Asian accent:

'Who is this?'

'Oh I'm sorry, can I speak to Salim please.'

'Why? Who are you?'

'Linda.'

'Linda who? What you want?'

'Excuse me?'

I couldn't handle it anymore and burst out laughing.

'You're such a prick.'

She was laughing too.

'How did you know it was me when I picked up?'

'Cos I could tell!'

'But everybody says hello the same way, you can't tell who's talking.'

'Of course you can, I knew it was you didn't I? Anyway, just don't do that again.'

'How's things?'

'Alright, dad's gone out, mum's doing the ironing. What are you doing?'

'Watching the news.'

'Please don't start any fights with Ranjit,' she must have been watching the news as well. 'You'll all starve if he gets pissed off and leaves.'

I peered round into the kitchen, he was moving a roti around on the tawa, the rest of them were still watching tv.

'Don't worry no one is starting anything.'

'So with this war going on are you still planning to go see your mum?'

I had decided after two years I'd go back for a visit. I had saved enough for a flight with some to spare.

'Yeah it's fine, there's nothing going on in West Pakistan.'

'If you say so. Just be careful regardless.'

'I will.'

'Will you miss me?'

'Maybe.'

'You're so unromantic.'

'I'll miss you like the bulbul misses the rose.'

'What's that supposed to mean?'

'I don't know it's used a lot in love poetry, I never quite understood the relationship.'

She chuckled.

'What's a bulbul?'

'It's a small bird that sings at night.'

'Oh a nightingale.'

'Maybe yeah.'

'Bulbul. Maybe I'll call you that from now on.'

'Guess you'll have to be rose then.'

'Fine by me, Rose is a much nicer name than Linda, and I definitely don't want to be called Bulbul.'

We laughed together until there was a silence between us.

'I'll miss you Bulbul.'

'I'll miss you Rose.'

'Will you send me a postcard?'

'Sure.'

'Tell me you love me.'

'I love you.'

'Was it really that hard?'

I always thought people only told each other that in films, I had never heard anyone say they loved anyone or anything. The word was reserved for Bollywood films and corny songs. But it was important for Linda, that was one of things I liked about her, she made me say and do things I would otherwise never do. She showed me a part of myself I would have otherwise never known.

'You have no idea.'

'Piss off.'

We laughed again.

'OK you can hang up now.'

'I was wondering when you'd let me go. Don't cheat on me while I'm gone.'

'I'll try.'

'Bye sweetheart.'

She exhaled through her nose.

'Bye.'

I put the phone back on the receiver and made my way back to their kitchen where they were serving the food and passing around the roti.

'Don't look so sad *yaar* you'll see her when you get back,' said Tariq as he passed me a plate of aloo gobi.

'I'm not sad, I'm fine.'

'Whatever *yaar*,' said Humayun. 'I've never seen your face so long.'

Maybe I did look sad, maybe because I was.

'What time is your flight tomorrow?' asked Ranjit.

'Eight in the morning'

'You want me to take you?'

'No, Mawlana already offered.'

'What does he think about Linda?' asked Humayun as he

placed a piece of roti wrapped around a chunk of potato into his mouth.

Tahir gave him a stare.

'He doesn't know,' I snapped back. 'And don't tell him either'.

'Relax, I'm messing around.'

He chuckled with his cheeks full of food as he turned to the other guys, but they weren't forthcoming in laughing with him.

'You know your mother might ask you to get married.' said Tariq.

The mood in the room became sombre all of a sudden, they looked at me expectantly to see what I would say.

'No, she wouldn't.'

'You're at that age now Salim,' Tariq continued. 'In our culture this is the usual time we get married. I was younger than you before I got married.'

The law had just changed so that people working in Britain could bring their families to join them. Tariq was in the process of bringing his wife and daughter to live with him, he was waiting to hear from the Home Office any day.

'Yeah I know, but I don't want to get married.'

'You know how it is Salim,' Tahir joined in. 'Once our parents decide something for us it's very difficult for us to go against it.'

'You've had your fun now Salim,' Humayun hadn't stopped putting food in his mouth but still managed to find space to talk. 'Let Linda go, and marry a nice girl from back home and start a family. Do you think Linda's family will accept you? Do you think your family will accept her?'

* * *

I had forgotten how hot it was here. I stepped out of the plane and the dry heat and its familiar smell hit me as soon as I made my way down the stairway. I had decided to wear my brown suit again, I could feel the sweat building under my shirt.

I went through immigration, picked up my suitcase and made my way out of the main doors to find Munny straight ahead of me, smiling and waiting. He hadn't changed a bit and it felt good seeing him. We had the mandatory awkward Pakistani man-hug and the argument of who would carry the suitcase. He won of course. It didn't take us long to get out of the city and into the countryside on the way back to the village. The car bumped and swayed as it made its way across the familiar potholes, it felt strangely familiar and at the same time unwelcome after having become used to the smoother roads in London.

'It's really cold in England isn't it?' asked Munny breaking the silence.

'What?'

'Cold in England, isn't it?'

'Oh, yeah.'

I felt sorry for not paying much attention to him since I had arrived. He was like a little child stuck in a grown man's body when he met me at the arrivals lounge, I could tell he was giddy with excitement, but trying to hold it in. His familiar grin seeming somehow wider than ever before. He asked a question every now again but I wasn't being very reciprocal, he didn't seem to notice, or care.

'Do you get our food over there?'

'What?'

He still hadn't realised my mind was somewhere else.

'Our food, do you get it over there, or do you have to eat white people food?'

'No we get our food over there.'

'Oh good.'

The old Radio Pakistan billboard came into view in front of us, it had been there since I could remember. Over the years the bright green slowly faded into grey and the writing in Urdu was vanishing. You wouldn't notice its decline if you saw it every day, you'd just look up at it every now and again and notice it had gotten worse since the last time you had bothered to look at it. Not having seen it for two years I noticed its deterioration more than I did when I saw it every day. Apart from the slow ageing of everything, nothing had changed, the same buildings stood in the same places, and the same familiar faces I'd see fade past on the way back from college were the same now.

'Nothing has changed,' it was the first thing I said to Munny all day that wasn't a response to a question.

'Oh nothing ever changes here. It's not like what we read in the news. Apart from this war a million miles away.'

'Let's hope my Bengali co-workers don't stop talking to me.'

'Are there Indians where you work as well?'

'Yes, many.'

'They don't start any trouble do they?'

'No, they're very nice people. I even live with a Hindu.'

'*Han?* Really? What's he like.'

'Very nice, very good cook.'

'Don't Hindus put cow piss in their cooking?'

'No. Well, not this one at least.'

'*Acha*,' he bobbed his head.

I felt disappointed in Munny for his presumptions. But then I thought if I hadn't moved to England and someone told me something silly about Hindus I would have probably believed them. Who am I to judge Munny just because I've lived in England for two years?

As we entered the village, it felt like it was completely deserted, there was not a single person to be seen.

'Where is everyone?'

'I don't know,' he replied.

His head bob was more accentuated than usual, I could tell he was up to something. As we turned the corner leading up to the house a large crowd had gathered blocking our way.

'What the hell is this?'

'I don't know,' came the same monotonous reply with the same head movement.

Now I was certain something was up, Munny showed no hint of surprise. I looked at him as he kept driving slowly towards the crowd, his familiar grin on his face, but that was accentuated too. As we drew closer the crowd parted and the sound of out of tune trumpets started blaring, a large banner was hoisted up as if it were for some political rally, it read "Welcome Salim Khan". As we drove through the crowd large beaming smiles peered through the window as they threw rose petals onto the car. What the hell was all this?

We slowed to a halt as we approached the house, the music came to a deafening crescendo, as drums started joining in with the trumpets. I got out of the car and was greeted with a garland of roses around my neck, with some petals into the face for good measure. As I made my through the crowd towards the familiar door, Ami and Abbas were waiting laughing with good measure at my expense.

'What is all this?'

Ami moved forward as though she hadn't heard my question and kissed my forehead.

'It's good to finally have you back, we've all missed you so much. As you can see!' As she motioned to the crowd the music stopped. 'This was Munny's idea.'

'Oh no,' Munny said as he made his way from the car. 'When I told people I was going to the airport to pick up *sir jee* everyone decided to welcome him back properly. When they all thought I would shuttle all of them to the airport I told them do what you want to do here, I'm not taking the whole village!'

'I don't know what the problem was,' said one of the old men in the crowd, a farmer in a stained white t-shirt and coloured sarong, his white moustache contrasting with his darkened skin from decades of working in the hot sun. 'If you would let us some of just sit on the roof it wouldn't have taken you that long.'

'The best thing about living in England *sir jee*,' Munny said as he shook his head. 'Is you get to run away from our crazy old men and their crazy ideas!'

The crowd laughed, the old man smiled wryly as he shook his head at the same time.

'It doesn't matter now,' Ami interjected. 'The young man is home and you all got to meet him. Come there is shikanjabeen and mithai for everyone. Take some and then go back outside to let the next group in to have some.'

We moved into the house and the crowd followed us enthusiastically inside, I wondered how many had actually come to just be treated. The rest of the day was spent with most of the village squeezed into the front courtyard spilling into the road, everyone chatting away, a welcome break away from the fields for most of the farmers. Some took it as an opportunity to raise their concerns and complaints with Ami, most just took it as a chance to ask me about life in England.

'I hear it's so cold your piss freezes in the morning.'

'I'd love to go myself, but I hear you have to eat pork and drink alcohol if you live there, is that true?'

'Is it scary to fly in a plane?'

I sat all day in one of the old lounge chairs, making the most of the warm sun beating down on my face, answering all the weird and wonderful questions they had. Most of the men hardly ever left the village, and when they would, it would only be for something important in their lives. Most of them sat on the floor around me listening to everything I had to say, like I was a wise elder. Almost all of them were older than me and had lived a life as long as mine many times over, it was awkward to say the least.

As sunset began to approach the call for prayer began to sound out and the villagers slowly started to make their way back to their homes. Those who prayed would stop by the mosque on the way, those who didn't would pretend they were going home to. Either way they all needed to get home before it became dark. They made their farewells, taking special care to greet Ami, they all wanted to make sure they were on her good side, even if she wasn't their landlady. After they had all left a silence filled the house.

'I thought they were never going to leave,' Ami had closed the door behind the last of them and made her way back in. 'I told Munny not to tell anyone you were coming, but he can never help himself if someone asks him about anything.' She sat down in the chair next to mine. 'Anyway it doesn't matter now, how are you son?'

'Good, how are things here.'

'Fine, the same as they always are. People always finding things to complain about.'

There was a momentary silence, the thoughts I had been

having the entire journey crept back into my mind.

'Is everything OK?'

She must have sensed something was bothering me. She used to call it "mother's intuition".

'Yeah everything's fine,' I lied.

'Well I'm sure you're tired, go to bed and we'll catch up in the morning.

I nodded my head and gratefully accepted the offer. I needed to rest and clear my head, I needed to get rid of this sense of dread I was feeling somehow.

* * *

Trying to sleep brought me no respite. I lay on top of my old charpai, its rope strung surface now unfamiliar to me, looking at the ceiling fan spinning away, illuminated slightly by the old yellow light Ami left on in the courtyard. I was thinking about Linda, I missed her and really wanted to hear her voice.

I got up and unlatched the door to enter into the night, cool air enveloped me and it was a relief from the stuffiness of inside, the doors were always kept shut at night to stop mosquitos coming in. It was early summer, and though the days were warm the night was mild, the air tingled my skin and the earthy smell of dew filled my nostrils. As I walked out into the courtyard I looked up at the moonless sky and saw all the stars shining, I had forgotten all about them, you don't see stars in London, I had never realised they had gone missing. Just like I had left the stars here I felt like I had left a different part of me back in England.

I heard movement behind me from one of the other bedrooms, a latch creaked open and clicked behind me, Ami came outside a shawl wrapped around her.

'Salim, what's wrong? Why are you standing out here?'

'I haven't seen the stars in so long.'

'What?' she asked confused.

'The stars, you don't see them the same way in England. There's only a few here and there, you don't see as many as you do here.'

'Well, I suppose that's at least one thing that makes us better than England.'

She was trying to be funny, in her motherly kind of way.

'Are you OK? Or are you just tired?'

'I don't know. It's strange being back here,' I said, still staring up at the sky.

'Strange to be back in your own home?'

Home. Could a person have more than one home? I had heard the saying on TV: "Home is where the heart is". What the hell did that even mean? If your family and your love are in two different homes then which one is your real home? Where do you choose to go sleep at night?

'Maybe I am just tired.'

'Go to sleep son. You'll feel better in the morning.'

I nodded my head and continued to look out at the night sky. She retreated back into her room, as I listened to the symphony of the crickets in the fields, a gentle cooling breeze washed over my face.

*** * ***

The heat in the morning was intense. We sat in the shade in the courtyard having channa puri for breakfast, my favourite. Usually it was reserved for the weekends, but I had come back at the beginning of the week and Ami couldn't wait. She was under the impression I hadn't had it while I was away, which wasn't true,

Ranjit made it on weekends sometimes too, and his was just as good as Ami's, but I didn't tell her that.

'What are the schools like?'

Abbas sat in his white school uniform, happy to have a special breakfast on a weekday that made a change from his usual bread and jam. Just like everyone else he was also keen to ask as many of his never-ending questions as he could.

'I don't know I haven't been to any of the schools.'

'Does everyone wear suits and bowler hats?'

'No.'

'What do they wear then?'

'Just normal clothes.'

'Do they wear suits at home?'

'No.'

'That's enough,' Ami interjected. 'Munny is outside, wash your hands and go, you're going to be late.'

She cleared his plates as he washed his hands abruptly in the kitchen, grabbed his bag and ran out to the wicket gate where Munny was standing behind as he opened it. Once she had cleared his crumbs away she sat down as I continued eating.

'Do you feel better?'

I had forgotten about last night.

'Oh yeah, fine. I think it was just jet lag.'

'I see.'

I realised from her slightly perturbed face that she was trying to hide that she must have never heard the term jet lag before.

'What are your plans for today?'

'I don't know, maybe see Imran and some of the other guys. I was thinking I might see Mawlana Ahmed's family.

'How is he?'

'Fine, his usual.'

We both smiled knowing that meant his old usual eccentric self.

'Why don't you take it easy today? Once you're fully rested you can go see who you need to see.'

I had forgotten how capricious she could be. Less than a minute ago she asked me what my plans were and the next she tells me to cancel them. I had gotten used to doing whatever I wanted in London without her checking up on me constantly. This would take some getting used to again.

'I say sir, it's very good to see you grace us with your presence once again.'

Imran walked in without either of us realising. He looked the same, except his hair was longer and more slicked back than before.

'Nobody told me James Dean was in Pakistan,' I said, referring to his new hairstyle.

I stood up to give him the traditional awkward Pakistani man hug that was usually reserved for Eid.

'You do know James Dean is dead right?'

'Seems like he's just been hiding in our village in Pakistan.'

We both had a good laugh at the expense of his hair.

'Sit down son,' Ami began the expected formalities. 'Have some breakfast, there's channa puri.

'Thank you aunty,' he said tilting his head to the side and putting his hand to his chest. 'But I've had breakfast and I need to get the bus before it leaves. I just came to say salaam before I left.'

'Come on I'll walk you to the bus.'

I made my way to wash my hands.

'Salim, are you sure you want to go out right now? You should get some rest.'

'I'll be fine.'

'What's wrong with him?' asked Imran. 'Has he gotten too used to the English weather?'

'I don't know, I don't think he's feeling too well.'

'I'm fine,' I interjected. I didn't even bother to dry my hands. 'Let's go.'

I was already on my way out before Imran realised.

'OK aunty I guess I'm going. *Khudhafiz.*'

Imran rushed out as I was already outside, the sun hit me harder than I thought it would.

'What was that all about?'

'Nothing, I needed some fresh air and you have a bus to catch. Let's get going.'

We made our way down the same track we did hundreds of times and it was already too familiar. As if the two years that had past were nothing, and all my friends and time in London were a dream. When I thought about Linda I had the same feeling you get when you wake up from an amazing dream only to realise it wasn't real. But she *was* real, and in that moment I couldn't wait to be with her again, like being able to get back into that dream you never wanted to end.

'So, did you get lucky with any ladies?'

And just like that my moment was ruined.

'They're not as good as your sister,' I said.

Imran stopped in his tracks while I kept walking.

'Woah, what happened to you?'

I stopped to look at him.

'What do you mean?'

'You would never make a joke like that.'

I thought about it for a second, and he was right. I was so used to being around mostly single older guys for so long I had forgotten what I used to consider was off limits.

'You're right I'm sorry. Let's go come on.'

'Are you OK. Your mum said you weren't feeling well.'

'I'm fine, you know how she is. How are you doing?'

'Waiting for you to send me a damn visa that's how I am.'

He was back to normal and no longer offended.

'What do I look like the Home Office?'

'My parents are still on me about finishing the degree,' he explained. 'But once it's done, do you think I could find work?'

'Yeah, there's plenty of work. But it's not fun, spending all day on your feet putting parts onto a car. If you ask me my opinion you might as well save the money on your degree if you're just going to work in a factory all day.'

'But it's only temporary right? We'll come back and use the money we saved and do something better.'

'Do you know anyone who's ever come back?'

I didn't want to have this conversation again. Imran was silent for a moment, our steps scrunching the ground beneath us.

'No, but, people have only just started moving there for work. They will come back. Won't they?' he asked a little unsure.

Guess I had no choice but to have this conversation.

'They've started letting people bring their families to live with them. One of the guys I live with is bringing his wife and kids soon. What do you think?'

'Everyone you talk to says it's just temporary.'

'They all say it, and they all want to come back. But I don't think it's going to happen.'

'You don't think you'll come back?'

'I don't know,' I didn't want to tell him about Linda, not yet anyway. 'I still want to, but honestly I don't know.'

'Does your mum know?'

'No! Let's keep it that way.'

We had arrived at the bus and I greeted the familiar faces that I knew. Some of them even came off the bus to greet me to the chagrin of the driver who had other pickups to make before heading to the city. All the usual questions were being asked about life in England and when I would come back to finish my studies. I brushed them off with the usual small talk.

The driver blared his musical horn, he was reaching the end of his tether with waiting. The boys said their farewells until it was just Imran left.

'How long are you here for?'

'Not sure just yet. Maybe a week or two.'

'OK. Well you should come over later, Ami and Abu would be happy to see you after so long.'

'Yeah inshallah I might come over.'

'Take care brother.'

He ran onto the bus before the driver left without him. With a screech and grunt it drove off into the distance leaving a trail of dust behind it. The boys at the back waved through the rear window as they got smaller. The sound of the tires and engine rumbled off into the distance and I stood watching it disappear until eventually all that was left was the sound of a cricket somewhere in the nearby grassland.

I could have been on that bus today, just like every other day. But things turned out different. Did I make the right decision? Would life have been easier to have just got on with what I had, and not travel half way across the world to work in a cold land in a colder factory all day long? Would it have been worth the sacrifice of never having known Linda, to be leading a less complicated life? I wouldn't have to go through the complication of explaining to Ami about Linda. I wouldn't have to tell her I wasn't going to marry a Pakistani girl of her choosing, someone who would look after her the way she looked after her mother-in-law, wear shalwar kameez and talk to her in her language.

I stood there alone and deserted. Trying to push away all these feelings and not dwell on them, but I just couldn't.

* * *

I walked back into the house closing the squeaky padlock behind me and found Ami preparing lentils.

'You took longer than I thought you would.'

I stood in the door and didn't say nothing.

'Salim,' she looked at me while she kept spreading the lentils in a plate. 'What's wrong?'

'Can I talk to you about something frankly.'

'Of course.'

She went back to her preparations. We had never had a real serious conversation about anything, she wasn't expecting one right now.

'I met someone that I want to marry.'

She stopped, now she realised it was serious.

'In England or here?'

'England.'

'A Pakistani?'

'No.'

'An English girl?' She had a look that was honest confusion. 'How did you meet her?'

'We both work at the factory.'

'Girls work there in factories with men?'

'Yes, well no. She works in the office.'

'OK. But, Salim I'm really confused.'

She put down her plate and put her hand to her lips thinking about what to say next.

'First of all, we decided that you were going to come back eventually. Is she going to come and live here in the village with us?' she asked the question already knowing the answer.

'No.'

'Then you're going to stay in England longer?'

'Yes.'

'For how long?'

'I don't know.'

'What would her parents think?'

'They know about us. I've met them.'

'Salim, I didn't take you for someone who would go chasing after girls.'

'I didn't go chasing after anything. We met and we...' I

didn't want to say we fell in love, that was so cliché, people in Pakistan never used the word. 'We just got on with each other.'

'So you're friends?'

'We're more than friends.'

She walked past me and sat down in one of the lounge chairs in the courtyard. She stared pensively at the ground, I could tell she had loads of questions she wanted to ask.

'Salim, fine you have this relationship with this girl, but getting married to her is something completely different. They're totally different to us. Their language, their way of life, their culture, their food. You have to spend the rest of your life with this person. Are you sure you want to do that?'

'Yes.'

'Salim, it's just, so strange. No one in our family has ever gone against our traditions like this.'

'So what?'

'What would people think? What will they say?'

'Why do you care? You're a single woman who bosses around farmers whose own wives and daughters never make a sound.'

'That's different.'

'No it isn't. Who else in our family does that?'

'I did it out of necessity.'

'Just…I want to marry this girl. If you don't want to give me your support, then fine.'

'You've always done what I've said, always been a good boy.'

She had a bad habit of being patronising when she didn't mean to be.

'I've not done anything wrong. I just want to marry someone of my own choosing.'

'I should never have sent you to England. I should have kept you here.'

'Well you didn't, and now it's too late.'

We didn't say anything. I stood there and she sat in the chair. It felt like we were there for five minutes but it couldn't have been for that long.

'I need to get back to the cooking,' she said matter-of-factly.

She went back to the kitchen and began to clatter the metal dishes. I had said what I needed to say. It brought me no relief, my anxiety had been replaced with regret. Not in having spoken the truth, but to have to put her through this. To put her through a situation she didn't know how to react to, how to deal with. Stuck in a world of traditions and norms she couldn't let go of, the only world she knew, and now something had come into it and she didn't know what to do about it.

* * *

'Why are you leaving so soon?'

I turned from my open suitcase where I was putting a shirt back in to see Abbas standing in the doorway, the sunlight beaming in from behind him.

'I have some things I need to sort out in England,' I lied to him.

'But you've only just come back after two years. Can't you get someone else to take care of it for you?'

'No, it's important and only I can do it. I'll try my best to come back soon.'

'When will that be?'

'I don't know.'

It had been a couple of days since I told Ami about Linda, and nothing had changed since then. Quiet moments sitting around the table, no conversation being had. I couldn't take the awkward silences anymore, there was no point to me being here any longer.

I closed the suitcase and fastened the straps after the last piece of clothing was back in. I made my way past Abbas who had now fallen silent sensing I didn't want to carry on our conversation. The sunlight was oppressive and bore down on me as I entered the courtyard, Munny was standing expectantly, car keys in hand, Ami sat on one of the lounge chairs idling her cup of tea staring into space. I placed my suitcase on the floor in front of her and waited for her to say something, but she retained her silence, and her stare into nowhere. I waited for what felt like an eternity before she turned towards me.

'God protect you,' was all she could muster. It was her standard farewell when we would leave the house.

'*Khudafez*,' was all I could respond with.

'*Allahafez*,' she took a sip from her tea and carried on staring into the spot in the corner.

Munny came and picked up my bag, I waited for a moment to see, to hope, there may be something further but I knew there would be nothing. I turned to Abbas and gave him a half smile, he looked down at the ground and couldn't meet my gaze. He could tell there was something amiss between me and our mother, but he was too young to understand or to comprehend what it could be. There was nothing left to do but leave.

Leaving the village, there was no fanfare, no goodbyes from the crowd that had greeted me just a few days before. They probably didn't even know I was leaving so soon. I didn't say anything to Munny until we arrived at the airport. He put out his hand to shake mine but I instead put my arms around him, I could tell he was taken aback by the stiffness in his body, but it subsided and he patted me on the back with the hand he just stretched out. I let go and met his smiling gaze.

'Look after them,' I said to him.

He wagged his head.

'Of course *sir ji*, but before you leave can I just say something?'

It felt like for the first time in our lives we were being formal with each other somehow. I looked at him expectantly.

'Every family has its ups and downs, this is life. If we don't share our worries and hopes with our family, then who will we share them with? It's the fact you can have an argument with people you love and the next day you can carry on like nothing happened, is a sign that we truly love them.'

To say I was taken aback was a major understatement. I had known Munny my entire life and had never heard him say anything so intelligent. I didn't know he had it in him.

'Thanks Munny. I never knew you never knew you were such a wordsmith.'

He put on his familiar sheepish smile and bobbed his head.

'Mawlana Ahmed used to say to me when I was a child, "Son, talk too much and no one will listen. Be silent and everyone will have open ears."'

I had forgotten that Mawlana Ahmed had also been Munny's religious teacher when he was a child, hearing his name made me look forward to seeing him when I got back to England.

'Thanks Munny, for everything. I'll be back I promise.'

'Inshallah.'

I tried to match his smile, but I don't think anyone in the world could at that moment.

'Inshallah.'

As I sat in plane and watched Lahore fade away from the ground I began to wonder if I was going to come back at all? I was going to marry Linda, I was sure of it, even if Ami still couldn't sit with the idea. But would that mean I would never come back? It couldn't be could it? This is where I was born, this is my home, my country. All these thoughts rushed through my mind and left a sour feeling in my stomach, the feeling of regret, of worry. I closed my eyes and tried to empty my mind, I tried to see Linda's face, her brown hair, the smell of them, her light green eyes reflecting in the sunlight. But the longer I focused on her, the image of Ami sitting in the morning light, her sad face staring into the distance kept coming back to me. All I could think about was her sitting there, as if mourning for something she's lost. And it kept haunting me. I gave in to it, and cried.

CHAPTER 11

Present

This incessant back and forth was doing my head in. I had a flight search engine on my phone screen and I wanted to fly out as soon as possible. But every time I did something the price would become inflated.

Today was a Wednesday, so I chose a flight out for tomorrow, it told me it would cost £350 with Emirates with a three hour stop in Dubai. OK great, I would just need a few days in Pakistan, so I chose a return on Sunday. But when I selected the return date it was now telling me the flight was costing well over a £1000 with a 30 hour stop in Istanbul with Turkish Airlines.

'God damn it!' I slammed the phone down on the desk. A rare moment of exasperated anger from me. The photos I had just propped up on the desk fluttered onto the floor and I couldn't catch them in time.

'Salim!' Linda was now standing at the bottom of the attic stairs, she had been talking to Wasim on the phone in the bedroom. 'What's the matter?'

'Nothing! I just…had a technical problem.'

'He says he had a technical problem,' she said to Wasim. 'Yeah I know,' she lowered her voice thinking I wouldn't be able to hear her. 'I think you should come over when you can, he's upset and bottling it all up.'

I picked up the photos off the floor, one was of our wedding, a black and white photo of us outside the registry office, me with my old brown suit, Linda in green short-sleeved dress. I could see the tufts of Mawlana Ahmed's turban on the left side next to me in the photo. He had insisted he perform the religious ceremony right after the civil ceremony, much to the bemusement of the registrar, and all of us really. His hurriedness in reducing the amount of time we were married legally and not married religiously was quite funny on the day.

The other photo was a faded colour one of us outside the first garage we had opened together. Linda was wearing green again, she had a bump from when she was pregnant with Wasim.

I stood the photos up again next to each other so all of faces were staring at me. It felt like our younger selves were looking at me with a veneer of a smile, that they were waiting for me to tell them what I was going to do next.

I picked up the phone and started my search again.

CHAPTER 12

1974

The shop door swung open and the bell rang to announce a new arrival. Linda looked up from the counter to see a middle-aged man in a beige parka jacket walk in, although it was sunny and mildly warm outside, the last remnants of summer were to soon start fading away. She gave him a warm smile which he reciprocated.

'Y'alright love, I need to get the oil changed in a Cortina if it's not too much bother.'

'Sure,' she replied. 'If you take a seat one of the mechanics will take a look for you once they're free.'

'Cheers love.'

As he turned around to take a seat he noticed the baby bump Linda placed her hand on gently.

'You look like you're about to burst!' he said laughing.

'Oh it's a stubborn one like his dad,' she looked down at it and rubbed it affectionately. 'He's taking his time.'

The man nodded his head as he looked through the window into the workshop where Salim and Ranjit were inspecting the inside wheel of a Morris Marina with a torch.

'How come the owner doesn't employ English workers

here?'

'Excuse me?'

'Why doesn't the owner employ English workers? They do a much better job than these lot.'

'Is that right?'

'Yeah, back in the old days, all the stuff we used to make in this country used to work a lot better, before we let all these lot start taking our jobs.'

Linda hesitated for a moment, a thought crossed her mind and she gave out a wry smile.

'Well if you like you can take it up with the owner, he'll be out in a moment.'

'Yeah you know what, I think I will.'

❈ ❈ ❈

I wiped my hands on a grimy cloth and made my way to the office, leaving Ranjit to resolve the problem with the Marina. I let the loose door swing behind me and shut itself as it silenced the machine Ranjit started up to use on the car.

'Don't know what he's done with it,' I said to Linda as I started rummaging for the order summary sheet. 'He must have been driving it like a bloody race car.'

As my rummaging lead closer towards her I went to sneak in a kiss. Linda moved away slightly and nodded towards the man sitting in the waiting area, who was failing at masking his surprise.

'There's a customer waiting,' she said matter-of-factly. 'He needs to get an oil change, he also has a suggestion he'd like to make.'

Salim made his way over to him smiling and held out his

hand.

'Hello mate,' I said with my deliberate mix of a cockney and Asian accent. 'I'm Salim, Sammy if you prefer, is there something I can help you with?'

'Um,' he slowly put out his hand to shake mine. 'No, it's OK Sal-, Sammy, I'd just like to get the oil changed in my Cortina please.'

'Ah right no worries. That's a standard oil change, I can do that for you now, is that it parked up front?'

'Err, yeah.'

'OK great bring it in and then Linda will sort you out with payment after we're done. Are you sure there was nothing else?'

'Err no, Just the oil change please.'

'OK great, bring it in.'

I turned around to make my way back to the workshop, I met Linda's eyes, she had a wry smile that told me what I needed to know. As the customer left and shut the door behind him it almost immediately swung open again, the bell rang to announce Mawlana Ahmed had arrived. He still wore his signature white shalwaar kameez and turban, but today, as the weather was starting to change, he wore a brown shawl around his shoulders.

'Asalaam alaikum!' he greeted us both.

'Walaikum salaam,' we responded in unison.

Mawlana Ahmed looked through the glass to see Ranjit working on the Marina.

'Ah I see you left the Indian to fix the problem, great, I'm never going to get it back now.'

'The Indian isn't the problem. It's your crazy driving.'

'What are you talking about?'

The customer with the Cortina made his way back in after

parking it next to Mawlana's Marina. As he walked back his exasperation at the sight of Mawlana became oblivious to all.

'You alright mate?' Mawlana asked him.

Now it was his turn to listen to Mawlana's hybrid accent.

'Yeah, fine,' he managed to say nodding.

'Alright, they haven't swindled you for too much have they?'

'Um, no.'

'Good, good! Makes a change innit!'

Mawlana, Linda and I laughed gleefully together, the gentleman managed to force through a hesitant smile.

'What are you doing to fix it then?' Mawlana turned to me switching to Punjabi making his way towards the shop floor.

'The question is are you going to stop breaking the thing so I don't have to fix it for free every month?'

I opened the door into the workshop for Mawlana, as I walked in after him I turned back to the other customer.

'Once I fix this Paki's car I'll change the oil in yours.'

'What did he say?' he asked Linda as the door swung shut.

'*Namaskar Swami Gee*,' Ranjit greeted him with his hands placed together.

They all burst out into laughter, though Linda couldn't understand the murmurs coming through the glass she got the gist of it and smiled. The man in the waiting area was still sitting in his chair, wondering what he should do.

* * *

As the last remnants of the sun began to disappear behind the darkening blue hue of the early evening sky, and mingle with the amber glow of the streetlights outside, Linda finally put away her financial register into the top drawer of her desk. As she closed it, Salim came through the workshop door, leaving it to swing shut behind him as he usually did. Ranjit shut the lights off in the workshop and brought the shutter down after himself leaving to go home. The sound of the radio was mixing in with the clamour of the garage being closed.

"Harold Wilson today returned to 10 Downing Street after securing a narrow victory for the Labour Party. He returns amidst the most uncertain economic period for Britain since the end of the war. With the country still feeling the effects of last year's oil crisis which resulted in a global recession and high inflation..."

Linda switched the radio off with a click.

'How does it feel?' she asked Salim. 'The first time you voted and your man won.'

'I thought we both voted Labour?'

'Well it's more important for you this time. Your first vote as a British citizen.'

'I just hope he does a good job and not waste my vote.'

'He was good for the working class the first-time round, let's just hope it carries on.'

'What did your dad vote in the end?'

'Don't know, don't care.'

Linda's relationship with her father had deteriorated after they got married. At first it seemed as though he was OK with the idea of them being together, but slowly things started to change and they started to grow apart.

'Has Ranjit gone home?' Linda asked.

'Yep,' I made my way behind Linda as she was clearing up her stationery, wrapped my arms around her and put my face next to hers. 'It's just you and me, what do you think we should do?'

Linda laughed and elbowed me gently in the side.

'Stop it, someone's going to see from the window.'

'We could just switch the lights off.'

'Oh, go away.'

I backed off smiling, and began to place the magazines in the waiting area back into a pile on the table.

'Salim, I've finished doing the accounts, we're not making much money.'

'Darling do you have to bring this up again? We're just starting out, once people find out we're not conmen and the word goes around we'll get more customers in.'

'It's not just that,' she moved from behind the desk and sat in one of the waiting room chairs, watching me clear away sweet wrappers left by children earlier in the day.

'Then what is it?'

'The weirdo who came in earlier, the oil change for the Cortina. He saw you and Ranjit in the workshop and said "the owner should hire English workers". It's not the first time someone's said something like that, people don't want to have work done by people who aren't English.'

'Well what do you want me to do?' my voice inadvertently rising slightly. 'Do you want me to put face paint on in the morning before I come in?'

'No dear,' she held my hand as I stared aimlessly at one of the magazines. 'I don't know. Maybe just hire at least one English guy.'

'You just said we're not making enough money, we can't afford to hire more hands. And after what you just told me, do you really think an English guy is going to take orders from a Paki."

I tossed the magazine onto the table and tried to moved away from Linda as she took up and her arms around me.

'OK I'm sorry, you're right, maybe hiring someone else just for their skin colour isn't the right thing to do.'

I held her hands as we just stood there.

'What's that thing Mawlana Ahmed says?'

'He says a lot of things a lot of the time.'

She laughed.

'The thing he says when he talks about the future.'

'Inshallah?'

'Inshallah everything will be OK.'

'Inshallah.'

I turned around and rubbed my hands on Linda's back and kissed her on the forehead.

'Let's just give it a few more months, we'll see how we do, if worse comes to worst me and Ranjit can always go back to working at the Ford factory. Let's just stick with the shop for now. People will come to their senses when they realise we aren't a couple of idiots off the boat.'

She gave out her nasal laugh and moved back to the desk to carry on clearing things away. As she moved about, I watched her brown hair uncurl around the side of her face. Despite all the things I knew she had to go through marrying me, the stares on the street, the inquisitive looks from strangers, the questions that were asked in silence. It was these moments when I knew I truly loved her. Because all those things didn't matter to her, they didn't show on her face, she didn't worry about it, the fact she loved me enough to be able to do all that was why I loved her more.

'Salim?'

'Yes dear,' I turned to face her and she had a pensive look, she had her hand on her bump.

'I think the baby is coming.'

CHAPTER 13

1974

Everything about this was the stereotypical scene from every film and TV show I'd seen. Man sits nervously outside, women screaming, nurses and doctors scurrying to and fro. I didn't realise how nerve racking the whole experience is, no matter how many times it's playacted for you.

'Mr Khan?'

I hadn't realised the door had opened, one of the midwives popped her head around the corner.

'You can come in now.'

I walked through the door to see Linda holding our son in her arms.

'Congratulations Mr Khan, it's a boy,' said the midwife as she closed the door.

'Thank you.'

I tried to hold back my tears, but they still managed to find their way through.

I kissed Linda on her forehead and looked at our son for the first time. There is nothing that comes close to the feeling of seeing your child for the first time. I had called Mawlana when we had arrived at the hospital to ask him to pray for us.

'Put your trust in God Salim, everything will be well. There is nothing that can describe being a father,' he had put on his serious hat, or should I say turban. 'It's like trying to describe the taste of honey. I cannot tell you in words the joy you will feel, just taste it and you will see.'

His own family were still in Pakistan and he hadn't seen them in years, though he didn't talk much about them, it was clear he missed them deeply. He was right, like he always was, there were no words to describe what I was feeling at that moment.

'Have you thought of a name?' asked the midwife.

'We decided that if it was a boy we'd name him after Salim's grandfather,' Linda explained. 'And if it was a girl it'd be after my grandmum. So I guess Wasim it is.'

'Aw that's a nice name. Something a bit different.'

I forced myself to smile. Wasim was a pretty common name for me, but I suppose maybe not for her.

I looked down at Wasim, happy at that moment, but also pensive about what our future held for us. Another human being's existence was completely dependent on us and we would do anything and everything for him. I had never thought I'd become a father and a husband in a place far away from where I grew up. I realised that his upbringing would be completely different to mine, but if he had been born in Pakistan it would have almost been completely the same.

I wasn't very religious but in that moment I prayed to God, just to make everything alright.

CHAPTER 14

Present

The sound of steps on the attic stairs brought me back to reality. I had found a photo of me, Linda and Ranjit in front of the shop on its opening day, I didn't know how long I had been staring at it wandering my way through the memories it brought me. I looked around to see it was Wasim coming up the stairs.

'Asalaam alaikum dad.'

'Walaikum salaam.'

'How are you feeling?'

'Yeah fine,' I said as I carefully put the photo back in its album.

'Mum told me about *dadhi*, she said you've been spending most of your time up here, are you sure you're OK?'

I turned to look at him and forced through a smile, he was wearing a white V-neck with jeans, the more I looked at him, the more I realised he began to resemble me when I was his age, aside from the beard where I used to have a moustache, and the fairer skin and lighter coloured hair he had picked up from his mother.

'Yeah I'm fine. I just decided to rummage through some

my memories that I had locked away.'

He looked at the old photo albums I had stacked around the desk.

'Come on dad, you can't just stay up here all day. You should get some air.'

'I'll come down in a little while. I just, came here to think for a bit that's all.'

He pursed his lips like his mother did when she wanted to say something but was hesitant to do so.

'Mum says you're thinking about going to Pakistan. Do you think that's such a good idea?'

I was a little disappointed Linda had told him, especially as I knew he would be averse to it.

'I have no choice. I need to go.'

'No you don't dad. It's not going to bring her back. You haven't been for so long, things are going to be completely different from what it used to be, and it can be really dangerous sometimes.'

'Weren't you the one who once told me not to believe everything the media says?'

'Well, sometimes they're not completely wrong all the time. You can't go by yourself you don't know anyone out there anymore.'

'Yes I do, I called your uncle Abbas earlier today.'

'Really?' He couldn't hide a mild sense of surprise. 'What did he say?'

'He told me to come home.'

'Come on dad, it's not really *home* anymore is it? I know it's where you came from but I'm just scared if anything happens to you. It's the stuff they don't tell you about in the media that I worry about.'

I looked at him wryly.

'Whatever happened to that T-shirt of yours that said "Child of the Diaspora"?'

I tried to ask it in an off-hand way, but it was obvious I was trying to highlight the fact he was worrying like a grown up, which was new for him.

'Dad, we're not exactly challenging postcolonial narratives here.'

Despite having been a suit and tie lawyer for so many years he was still at heart the radical liberal student.

'Nasima's dad's always telling me how dangerous the countryside can be,' he continued. 'If he didn't have to go back to check on the land his family owns he wouldn't go back at all. He says he feels like a walking bank ready to get robbed at any time. If you're really adamant to go dad, then I have to come with you, or at least go with Nasima's dad when he visits next.'

'You can't come with me when Nasima is expecting so soon.'

'Well can you not at least wait a couple of months?'

'No Wasim I can't, and I can't explain it but I just need to go now. I know you say you're worried, and I promise I will be careful, but I have to go.'

He let out a long nasal sigh, this time it was one of my habits. Linda told us we both did it when we knew we weren't going to win an argument.

'Why is it so important for you to go back? What will it achieve?'

I let the question settle in my mind for a moment, I needed to make sure I knew the answer myself.

'It was inevitable one day I would have to go back. It doesn't matter how deep you bury your past, it'll still grow back to remind you of what was once there. I can't explain why I feel the need to go back, the fact I have that desire in me means that some part of me won't be satisfied until it gets what it wants. And I feel like that part of me that's yearning for it so much *should* get what it wants. I don't know, none of what I'm saying makes sense, I guess I just can't describe how I'm feeling in words.'

'No dad, I think I know what you mean. I still don't think it's a good idea, but if your mind's made up I can't stop you.'

'If Nasima wasn't pregnant I would take you with me. But she needs you right now.'

'Alright,' he sat down on one of the old office chairs that had been dumped in the attic, his momentarily silence after a serious conversation meant he was waiting to say something funny. 'But if you get kidnapped I'm not paying your ransom.'

He had been thinking about whether it was the right time to crack a joke at his old man's expense. I was glad to lighten the mood a little bit.

'Why not?'

'I can't afford it right now with the baby on the way.'

'Oh right, so get rid of the old if you get the chance to make way for the young? Thanks!'

Wasim's smile brought respite to my mood and I felt the first bit of relaxation since I had received the letter.

'I always used to wonder if and when you would ever go back. Sometimes I would think you should go back more often to reconnect with who you are. Now that you're going I'm not so sure.'

'I would be lying if I said if I wasn't worried. But I'll try to be careful. I promise I'll come back in one piece.'

'Inshallah.'
'Inshallah.'

CHAPTER 15

1978

'We can't take Wasim with us can we?'

Linda looked at me pensively as I opened the door. More protesters were gathering together to make their way to the high street, and the commotion and chanting from that direction became louder now. I looked at Wasim and he looked up at us unsure of what was going on.

'It'll be OK, we'll stay back away from the main group of people.'

'Are you sure Salim?'

'We're doing this for him Linda, if we don't stand up now what future is he going to have?'

Linda's face turned to one of grit and resolve.

'Let's go.'

Altab Ali had been stabbed on his way to vote after leaving work, and the East End was angry. The local Bengali groups had coordinated a massive protest to march from Whitechapel to Downing Street. We didn't think much of it at first. It felt like there were protests every week, some by the National Front, other times by those confronting them. But that morning when we saw the streams of people making their way through the streets through the living room window, we felt like we had to do something.

As we made our way towards the high street the clamour became refined into chanting. "Black and white unite!", "The National Front is a Nazi front!".

'Even the West Pakistanis have come out," said a voice behind me in Urdu with a Bengali accent.

It was a couple of my old colleagues from the Ford factory, Mojib and Sheikh. We shook hands and smiled, it had been a long time since we had seen each other.

'This is my wife Linda and our son Wasim.'

'Oh Linda!' said Sheikh. 'I remember you from Ford, I didn't know you two got married.'

'Five years now,' I told him.

'Wah, amazing yaar!' said Mojib.

'How are you young man?' Sheikh asked Wasim. Wasim smiled shyly and embraced his mother's leg. 'You going to grow up and be like your dad huh?'

'Salim,' Mojib switched back to Urdu. 'I don't think it's safe for the boy. These Nazi bastards are crazy man. Maybe you should send them back home. Especially if they see you with an English woman who knows what they might do.'

Linda looked inquisitively at the two of us, she didn't understand but she got the gist of what we were talking about.

'Linda there's a lot more people here than we thought,' I attempted to feign ignorance. 'Maybe you should take Wasim home.'

'You're not going to come back with us?'

'It's OK Linda,' said Mojib. We will stay with him and look after him.'

Sheikh bobbed his head in agreement.

Linda looked at Wasim and then at the crowd. She wanted to protest, she wanted to stay in her place and make her voice heard. But it was her who had first hesitated in taking Wasim out, and now she had an opportunity to take him back and keep him safe.

'I'll see you back at home Salim.'

Linda and Wasim waded sideways through the crowd back to the pavement. I watched them fall away behind us as the progression of people kept moving forward.

'There's so many of us,' I said to them both. 'Would it really have been a problem?'

'Now is not the problem,' Mojib explained. 'Afterwards when everyone goes back home, there will probably be a counter protest.'

'Our people have never come together like this before. It's going to really piss them off.'

How things had changed in just under the ten years I'd been here. The 70s saw the rise of the National Front and every day there was always a chance you'd get called a name, or shoved, or spat at, or have something thrown at you. Linda and I would always get stared at when we left the home. We had decided to move somewhere further out towards Essex, we could feel the tensions rising and it was an environment we needed to get out of.

We reached the high street and the crowd had swelled to thousands of people, streams of them coming from the surrounding roads, holding up banners and chanting. Most of the crowd were Bengalis, but there was a mix of black, white, Indians and Pakistanis. The walk was long but time passed quickly. This was my first protest and the atmosphere was ablaze with anger and a demand for justice.

We reached Whitehall and stopped as the people at the head of the protest delivered a letter to the prime minister in Downing Street. The crowd then moved to Hyde Park Corner where speeches were delivered in a mix of English and Sylheti. Once all was said and done the crowd then went back the way it came returning to the East End.

'How is Mawlana Ahmed these days?' asked Sheikh.

Mojib's face brightened at the mention of his name. Many had fond memories of him and still remembered him.

'A mosque in Ilford offered him a job to be an imam,' I told them. 'Once he finishes there he does night shifts at the Plessey factory.'

'That guy never stopped working. Bloody machine yaar,' said Mojib.

As we turned a corner and broke away from the main group a gang of white youths were staring at us. Though we didn't say anything the mood changed and we tried to avoid their gaze.

'You pakis have a gay old time then eh?'

None of us said anything and kept walking. But the group moved towards us and blocked our way as we tried to make our way past. The leader came up to me and I met his gaze.

'You lot don't like being stabbed maybe you should just piss of then.'

'Just let us go home mate,' I said to him.

'Where's that then? Paki-land?'

A snigger rippled through the group. They then started to push us back the way we came.

'Oi!'

A shout come out from behind them. It was Dan, Linda's

old ex, with four other black guys who I recognised were also from Ford. I hadn't seen Dan since the wedding, this was a Ford reunion I wasn't expecting.

'Get yo rasclaat back,' he told the leader.

He had opted for his Jamaican accent today.

'Who the fuck are you? Fucking piss off the lot of you yardies.'

His challenge was met with a fist into his cheek from one of Dan's friends, at which they all flew into a rage of punches and kicks. Mojib took out a two-inch blade from his jeans pocket and thrust it into the back of one the boy's thighs and twisted it. He let out a piercing scream. He put his hand to where the blade had dug in and saw it covered in blood. As his friends turned to look at him, they realised they were in trouble. The Jamaicans pushed in on them and forced them to run into the main crowd on the high street.

'I thought family life would have kept you out of trouble,' Dan said breathing heavily, this time in his cockney accent.

'Trouble? Me? They started it!'

'I'm kidding brother!' he let out a chuckle.

He turned to Mojib and Sheikh.

'Oi oi. All the Ford boys coming out to party today.'

He shook hands with the two of them.

'Stay out of trouble boys. I'll see you around yeah? Give Linda my regards Sammy.'

'Take care of yourself Dan. And thanks.'

'No worries brother.'

Our two groups went separate ways in opposite directions, along the way Mojib dropped the knife into a gutter when no one was looking.

'You always carry that thing with you?' I asked him.

'Salim bhai,' he replied. 'You never worked night shifts at Ford, and now with your own garage you can shut up shop whenever you like. But you see what happened to Altab? It's dangerous after dark. I only keep something on me just in case I absolutely need it.'

Mojib and Sheikh left me in front of the house. We scrawled down each other's numbers and said our farewells after what seemed like the longest day. It was golden hour, and the sun was illuminating the grimy East End in all its glory.

'Daddy daddy!' Wasim came streaming down the hallway into my arms as I closed the door behind myself. Linda made her way from the kitchen and stopped, she looked at me worryingly.

'Salim, what happened?'

Uncertain what she meant I followed her gaze to my abdomen and I realised it was covered in blood, not mine, but from the guy Mojib stabbed. I looked at my palms and they were both covered in crimson red.

CHAPTER 16

1985

I hadn't realised the plane had even taken off. It was only when I heard the ding on the seatbelt light and there was a slight commotion of people around me that I found we were already in the air for quite some time.

"Brixton on Fire Again" was the headline for the day's paper that I had been reading. What followed was an attempted analysis in understanding what lead to the second riot in Brixton for four years. A pretty poor attempt by a middle-class white man who had never worked up a sweat at work in his life trying to figure out why the "coloureds" were angry.

We had seen the disregard the police had for us, Blacks and Asians (though back then we were all black). And there was no let-up in the racism going around, so Linda and I had agreed to move out to Woodford. A leafy green suburb which felt like it was a different country altogether let alone another part of London. Most of the Asians in Whitechapel preferred to use our garage so we had made enough money to afford a three-bedroom semi-terrace. Our next investment was to open another branch near to our new home, and let Ranjit run the Whitechapel garage.

❊ ❊ ❊

I jolted forward as the plane landed. I hadn't even realised I had fallen asleep again, and before I realised we had arrived. In just seven hours I was back to my old home which now felt like a new place.

Adverts outside the airport lauded President/General Zia's support of the mujahideen in Afghanistan, that was certainly new. I don't remember politicians taking out adverts giving themselves pats on the back.

I looked around for Munny but I couldn't see him. I scanned the crowd of people multiple times who just stared back at me with their empty gazes. It wasn't like him to be late. I didn't want to call home as I had told Munny not to tell anyone, not even Ami or Abbas that I was coming this time. But after waiting and waiting with no sign of him I had no choice.

I made my way over to a taxi desk next to a payphone and asked the bored guy behind the desk to break my ten rupee note into coins for me, which he seemed reluctant to do. I looked over to a seating area to my right and there he was. A newspaper was sprawled over his belly, he was slouched down in the low airport chair and was snoring away with his mouth wide open. He had aged considerably, he had little hair left and what was there was all white. I felt sorry in that moment for him, not just for having him drive out all the way to pick me up, but just for the fact he had aged so much. The jolly and bubbly Munny I knew from my childhood was ageing away.

The bored taxi desk man handed me my change, which I couldn't be bothered to change back now. I sat down in the seat next to Munny hoping some slight movement might wake him up gently. No luck.

'*Bhai saab*?' I said gently.

Nothing, just more snoring.

'*Bhai saab!*'

Munny came alive with a jolt.

'Can I get a cigarette?' I asked him.

'Cigarette? What are you talking about-'

He stopped and stared at me when he realised who it was. The old familiar smile from his youth broke through his tired and worn face.

'*Arre, sir jee*? Was your flight early?'

He looked down at his watch.

'No, it was on time for once,' I told him. 'But it looks like you were a bit too early.'

His smile changed to one of embarrassment.

'No it's not like that, I got here and saw the flight hadn't arrived so I sat down to read the paper, I must have fallen asleep after that.'

'It's OK, I'm in no rush. Do you want to finish off your nap before we head off?'

His ever-expanding smile widened further.

'*Arre* leave it yaar, *chalo*.'

The drive back was different for once. The potholes were bigger, that was one thing. And I didn't remember so many signs being up everywhere. Advertising looked like it had taken off in Pakistan: A mishmash of politics, Coca-Cola, Pepsi, and the odd washing machine brand.

'What's new Munny?'

He wasn't his talkative old self anymore, he hadn't said anything since we left the airport. I was starting to miss his questions and conversation. I never thought I'd say that to myself.

'What's new sir jee? Nothing,' he laughed. 'The roads are bumpier, as you can see, General Zia saab is helping the brothers in Afghanistan fight the Russians, and in return the *molvis* are telling people to support him. Everybody is starting to get religious now all of a sudden.'

'Is that right?'

'Yeah, all of a sudden everyone is praying now. My own son wanted to go to a madrassa to become a *hafiz*, the next thing I know he leaves me a letter saying he's gone to Afghanistan.'

I looked at him and could see he had become distressed and worried, though he tried not to show it, the ever so slight scowl he had was enough to tell me. I had never really known Munny's family, he spent so much time with us that I can't imagine how much they got to see him. If I didn't feel bad about him getting old, I certainly felt bad now about taking him away from his family.

'*Inshallah* he'll come back safe.'

The words were empty of course, I didn't know it to be true or not.

'*Inshaallah*, just keep him in your prayers.'

He hastily wiped away a tear. We carried on the rest of the journey in silence.

As we arrived to the house a nervous sense of anticipation started to cover me. How would they take my surprise visit? Would they be happy to see me without having made any preparations? As we turned the corner a new Honda was parked in front of the gate.

'Did you buy a new car?'

His old shy smile came back.

'No sir jee, I don't know who this could be.'

There was no one inside the car, they must have been in the house. Munny parked up in front of the neighbour's house, parking on the other side of the road next to the fields would have meant no one would have been able to pass.

'They know this is your mother's car,' referring to the neighbours. 'If they need to get out they'll just knock.'

I looked at the car and wondered who it could be. Some relatives coming to visit? I didn't know anyone who could afford a shiny new car like this.

Munny rattled the loose bolt on the door and waited for a response. Nothing for a while, then the familiar scraping of sandals on dusty slabs came approaching.

'Who is it?'

Was that Abbas? I didn't recognise the voice at all.

'It's me,' responded Munny.

He then switched places with me so that I would be the first person he'd see.

Abbas opened the door and didn't offer a glance at first, but when he realised Munny wasn't standing there he looked at me with mild shock. He had started to resemble me, minus the moustache, a lot skinnier, and pretty much the same height.

'Bhai?' he asked with a laugh. He vigorously shook my hand. 'When did you get here?'

'An hour ago, are you surprised to see me?'

'What kind of a question is that? Of course I'm surprised to see you. Come in yaar, what are you standing in the door for.'

We walked through to the seating area where Ami was sitting with an elderly couple, a man in a suit and his wife wearing a formal shalwar kameez.

'Ami, look who's here.'

She was wearing a formal shalwar kameez too, and then I realised they were all wearing smart clothes, Abbas too. I presumed they must be a *rishta* for Abbas, meeting him as a potential suitor for their daughter. Ami put on a shy smile that bordered on awkward, this wasn't the best time to make a surprise appearance.

'Asalaam alaikum,' I shook the man's hand and offered the same greeting to his wife.

'Walaikum salaam,' he responded gently. He peered at me through his round brass glasses. 'And you are?'

'Salim,' I thought it would have been enough of an answer but his curious look remained. 'Ami's eldest son.'

'Oh,' he turned to Ami. 'I thought you said you only had one son.'

I felt sick in my stomach. Ami laughed nervously.

'Yes, he is my sister's son, but I think of him as my eldest.'

The couple nodded their heads together, seemingly accepting her explanation.

I didn't make an effort to hide my change in mood which would have been apparent to them. I was fuming. Abbas looked at Ami which added to the unsubtle change of mood.

I walked away silently taking my suitcase towards my old room.

'Salim,' Ami called after me. 'Do you want to eat something?'

I closed the door behind me and said nothing.

❋ ❋ ❋

They had put a tv in my old room, everything else was pretty much the same as I had left it. The bedding, the charpoy, the little knick-knacks. I sat with my back against the wall, I hadn't bothered to change or unpack. Mehdi Hassan was performing on PTV, his low melancholic voice singing of yearning and loss, which just added a damper to my already bad mood. The guests had left around an hour ago and the sun had set. The only sound to be heard were the crickets chirping.

'Salim,' Ami knocked on the door gently.

I didn't respond, she opened the door slowly anyway and peered inside before coming in. I didn't look at her or say anything, just kept watching the television. She closed the door and stood in front of it.

'Salim, you have to try to understand. I'm trying to do what's best for Abbas.'

She waited for me to say something, I didn't.

'If I tell people about your family they might take it the wrong way.'

'What is there to take the wrong way?' I snapped at her. 'A man married a woman and had a child. Doesn't everyone in this damn country do that?'

'Yes, but they marry someone of their parent's choosing.'

I scoffed.

'So you'd rather I didn't exist than have to deal with what strangers think about your family.'

'This is the curse of our people. We're forced to live our lives by "*Lok kya kenghe?*"' What will people think? 'But what can I do?'

'Don't make excuses for yourself.'

'It's the truth, and you know it. You may not live here anymore but you're still a Pakistani. Don't tell me people in England don't say things about you and your wife?'

'They're not my mother.'

She looked down at the ground in a repose that veiled her pain. I felt remorse for what I said even though I didn't want to.

'I suppose I have failed.'

'That's not what I meant.'

'But it's what you feel right now.'

'Tell me how you would feel if you were in my position?'

'Tell me what you would do in mine?' she retorted. 'If I told that man I had an elder son, and he asks me if you're married-'

'Then say yes.'

'Then he will ask which family did we marry into.'

I didn't want to admit it but she was right. All these bullshit questions strangers asked that served no purpose but to massage people's egos.

'Just forget it.'

I laid down on the charpoy. I was tired from travelling, and from being angry, I didn't want to carry on this pointless conversation that would serve no purpose.

'Will you not eat something.'

Even after all this, she was still my mother, my stomach was still her biggest worry.

'I'm not hungry.'

She walked out and closed the door behind herself gently. The fan above me spun away in a hypnotic motion, Mehdi Hassan slowly lulled me into sleep.

* * *

The next morning we ate breakfast in silence. Ami had made channa puri, I assume as a peace offering, I wasn't interested.

'Are you going to see Imran?' asked Abbas.

'No.'

I took a sip from my chai and didn't bother saying anything more. He looked at me pensively, trying to choose his next question carefully. I felt sorry for him and decided to make an effort.

'Who's the girl?'

'Huh?' The question took him by surprise.

'The *rishta* from yesterday. Who are they?'

'Oh,' Abbas looked at the kitchen to see Ami clattering dishes away. 'She's a friend from university,' he said in a hushed voice. 'Ami doesn't know.'

I looked at him in surprise. Well this was interesting.

'How did you set it up?' I asked him a low voice.

'Her father, the man who was here yesterday, is a lecturer at the university we go to. I'm good friends with one of his colleagues, he's an uncle of one my classmates. We worked out a plan together where he told her father he knew someone who might be good for his daughter.'

'I see.'

He had certainly grown up, and had become more cunning than I would have thought.

'Well if it doesn't work out you can blame me for it.'

He shook his head.

'Come on bhai, it'll be fine.'

'Just don't run away together.'

He looked at me incredulously.

'Come on, what do you take me for?'

'These Indian films get more and more dramatic every year, who knows you might pick up some crazy ideas.'

His look was now dismissive.

'Come on, what do you take me for? And for your information I don't watch Indian films.'

'You being a hopeless romantic, I can just about get my head around. But a patriot who boycotts Indian films, not buying it.'

'What are you talking about?' Ami appeared without warning, sitting down in one of the chairs.

'Nothing,' we responded in unison.

The slight lull in my low mood came to an end. I wanted to talk to my brother more, to find out about this boy I once knew who was becoming a man.

'How long will you be here for?' Abbas asked, trying to change the conversation to something more suitable.

'I'm leaving tonight.'

'What?!' Ami carefully slammed her teacup down into its saucer.

'I called the PIA ticket office this morning, I rescheduled my flight for later today.'

'Salim,' Ami began. 'You just got here, you can't just leave in a day.'

'I'm not wanted here, so why bother staying.'

She put the cup and saucer down and stormed off to her bedroom. I had never seen her upset before, this was the first time I noticed her crack in her perpetually calm demeanour. There was a part of me that felt sorry, but another part of me that didn't want to care.

'Why did you do that?' Abbas asked me.

'What should I have done?'

'Talk to her.'

'We did.'

'Well, talk to her more,' he tried in vain.

'There's nothing more to talk about.'

'She's our mother, she made a mistake, give her some time, she'll realise what she did was wrong.'

'She knows what she did was wrong, but rather than apologise she'd rather try to justify herself.'

'You know how hard it is for her, raising us by herself, looking after the land. She's had to go through so much, and she made up one lie to try and make things a little easier for herself. Do you remember her ever lying to us before?'

Abbas made a compelling argument, yes it was true, I don't remember her ever lying to us about anything, not even about silly little things parents say to their children. And yes, she had a rough time being a single mother in a world full of men.

'It's not just her lying about me. Since I told her about Linda she has struggled to accept her for who she is, and by extension her grandson.' I decided to ask him the same question I asked Ami last night. 'Tell me if you were in place, what would you do?'

I looked at him straight in the face.

'I'd still try to make amends with her. Our religion doesn't allow us to break ties of kinship.'

I let out a chuckle.

'Didn't she do the same thing? Munny told me everyone is turning into a mullah these days thanks to Zia.'

'It's not a joke. I know you love and respect Mawlana Ahmed, he'd tell you the same thing.'

He had a point. He was the only person I took religious advice from seriously, and yes he would have used those exact same words. But it felt extra patronising coming from my younger brother.

'Whatever,' I tried to dismiss his preaching. 'What's done is done. I'm heading home.'

'This is your home.'

'It doesn't feel like it anymore.'

The gravity of those words felt like a shadow enveloping me. I scraped the chair back and stood up. I was done with this conversation, and done trying to be made to feel pitiful. I walked into the bedroom through the unopened door and picked up my suitcase, I hadn't unpacked, and then walked back to Abbas.

'Goodbye Abbas. I hope you end up marrying the girl.'

He looked at me and said nothing. I turned to look at Ami's bedroom. I couldn't see anything through the screen door but it felt like she was staring back at me through the darkness between us.

I unlocked the padlock on the door and stepped out into the late morning sun, it wasn't too hot yet. I moved to the side and waited for Munny to arrive. I had called him earlier on the telephone and asked him to take me to the airport, avoiding his questions. He showed up two minutes later. As I went to put the suitcase in the boot he rushed out.

'Is everything OK?' he asked worriedly.

I hadn't told him why I was leaving already, on top of that, we never waited for him outside, he would always come in to get us. It was unusual for him.

'Yeah, fine. Let's go,' I said abruptly.

On the drive to the airport we were both scowling for different reasons. He was apprehensive about why I was leaving so soon. I was scowling because my mind was bitter about the fact that two times I had come back to Pakistan, and each time I've had to leave with a sour taste in my mouth. I decided if this was how it was going to be, I wasn't coming back.

We arrived at the airport and hadn't said a word to each other. We both got out.

'Munny, don't wait for me to go through security,' I said to him as I took my suitcase out of the boot. 'Just go home.'

I took my wallet out, it was stuffed with Pakistani rupees and English pounds, I took out the whole wad and kept a £10 note and a few small rupees and handed the rest to him.

'If you ever need money, I want you to call me OK?'

He didn't want to take it.

'Sir jee...'

'Munny, I don't know if I'm coming back, just please take it.' I took his hand and pushed the money in. I grabbed onto the suitcase and looked at him. Despite his age I could feel the sadness on his face which made him look helpless. 'I'll make *dua* your son comes back inshallah.'

It had been a while since I had prayed, but I was being honest. I don't know what I would do if I ever lost Wasim the way Munny lost his son. He embraced me. It took me by surprise.

'Munny, it's OK yaar.'

He let go and looked at me straight in the face. He had tears in his eyes.

'I always considered you and your brother to be like my own sons. My father looked after your father, and I looked after you. You may not say anything about what you're going through, but I can feel your pain.'

He was right. He wasn't just a servant, in many ways he had come to replace our father after he had died, and became the rock which our family all relied on. I held his shoulder.

'I will miss you Munny. Thank you for everything you have done. *Khudhafiz.*'

I walked into the airport, feeling his gaze behind me as I moved further and further away from him, never to look back.

After going through all the airport rituals and after the flight had taken off. I went straight to the bathroom after the seatbelt light came off. I put the lid down and sat on top of the toilet with my face in my hands, and I cried. I cried like a baby, and all I could hear in my head was Mehdi Hassan, singing a song of yearning and sadness.

CHAPTER 17

1985

The school bell rang and the scream of children followed almost immediately afterwards. Linda sat in the waiting room outside the headmaster's office as the secretary rattled away at her typewriter, peering over her glasses at the page intermittently.

Linda rubbed her knuckles nervously. After years of doing clerical work, just like the school secretary, her hands constantly felt like they were wound too tight. Only a few weeks before she had found another grey hair at the front of her crown. For some reason she thought about the first time her and Salim had gone out on a date. Back when they were young and carefree without a worry in the world. Now it was a world of meetings with the headmaster, running a business, worrying about your bones, and finding the latest grey hair.

Mr Davids the headmaster opened the door. His thin white hair and fading tweed jacket made him look older than he actually was. Behind him Linda saw Wasim sitting on his chair facing out the long window behind Mr David's desk, bathing him in sunlight.

'Thank you for coming Mrs Khan, will you come in please?'

As Linda sat down in the chair next to Wasim he shifted his gaze to the floor, she placed her hand under his chin and tilted his face towards to see the redness around his eye.

'Was what you have done?'

'He was involved in an altercation with another pupil this morning,' Mr Davids told her as he sat down. 'The other boy had to be sent home. Mrs Khan this isn't the first time it's happened. Mrs Wise, his form tutor tells me Wasim is constantly getting into altercations with other pupils.'

'They always start it,' Wasim said in a low voice.

'It doesn't matter who starts it,' Mr Davids said abruptly. 'There's never a good reason for fighting your other classmates.'

'What do you have to say for yourself Was?' Linda asked him.

'They always say mean things to me, saying that you married a paki' he wiped at his eye. 'I got angry today because Tom was saying mean things about you and he wouldn't stop.'

'Why didn't you tell your teacher Was?'

'I always tell Mrs Wise but she doesn't care, she never does anything.'

'I assure you Mrs Khan, if Wasim had told his teacher she would have done something.'

'No she doesn't,' Wasim replied sheepishly.

'Mr Davids, have you asked Mrs Wise about the other boys? About what they say to Was?'

'Yes Mrs Khan, she tells me she's not aware of any bullying towards Wasim.'

'She's lying!' Wasim said louder.

Mr Davids let out a long sigh.

'Mrs Khan, as you can see I think Wasim has a problem

with his temper.'

'With all due respect Mr Davids I think I know my son's temperament better than most. And I don't see why he would be making something like this up. To me it sounds like Mrs Wise isn't taking Wasim's complaints seriously.'

'Mrs Khan, with all due respect, I have the utmost trust in all of my staff to take reports of bullying seriously.'

'I see.'

'The school disciplinary procedure is very clear that we will have to suspend Wasim for a week.'

'Is that necessary? This is the first time it's happened.'

'From what Mrs Wise tells she has had a number of conversations with Wasim regarding his behaviour, I think suspending him will be the only way he will learn his lesson. And besides, it's the school's standard policy, we can't make any exceptions.'

'And the other boy, Tom?'

'When he comes back into school I'll discuss with Mrs Wise and then decide what appropriate action to take.'

'You just said there is a standard procedure on disciplinary action.'

Mr Davids looked down at his desk and gave a condescending smile.

'Rest assured Mrs Khan, Tom will be punished as well. But given the injury Wasim afflicted on Tom a suspension is mandatory.'

'I see. Thank you for your time Mr Davids, rest assured I'll have a word with Wasim, this won't happen again.'

'I'm sure it won't,' he got up to move round to open the door. 'Thank you for you coming in.'

Wasim and Linda walked out and made their way along the corridor leading to the school exit, the long windows showed the playground was almost empty as most of the children had now made their way to class.

'Mum, I don't want to come back here. I keep telling them about the other boys picking on me but they never do anything.' Linda stopped to look down at her son. 'Please don't make me come back.'

'Was, if it were up to me I wouldn't bring you back here. But the next school is too far away to take you to in the mornings, I can't drop you off and get to the garage to open up in time.'

Wasim wrapped himself around her leg.

'Please don't make me come back,' he said into Linda's leg. She could feel the dampness of tears on her thigh, she placed her hand on the back of his head. A sense of regret entered her, the regret of having told her only child what neither of them wanted to hear.

'I'll talk to your father, we'll figure something out Was.'

'Do you have to tell dad?'

'Yes.'

'He's going to be mad isn't he?'

'No Was, it's not your fault. I'll talk to him I promise.'

❋ ❋ ❋

It was when I walked through arrivals at Heathrow that I really felt tired. I didn't sleep on the plane this time, and I didn't feel like I wanted to, but now all of a sudden the back to back flights were starting to take a hit on me. On top of that I was still bitter about what had happened, and my anger was now slowly dissipating to make way for regret for the brashness of my actions.

Ranjit stood waiting in front of the doors as I walked through them, his look was serious.

'What happened yaar?' he asked.

Straight to the questions, no messing around. We started walked together towards the car park.

'I don't want to talk about it.'

'OK.' He was slightly surprised by my bluntness, he wasn't used to me talking to him like this. 'I was just surprised you asked me to pick you up and not Mawlana saab, he's usually your airport guy.

'I don't want to tell him what happened.'

He looked at me with deadly seriousness.

'That bad?'

'Yeah.'

'What makes you think I won't do the same?'

'I don't. But at least you don't have my family's phone number.'

'I see.'

I could tell he wanted to say something funny, but it wasn't the right time.

'Who did you leave in charge of the shop?' I asked him.

'Dan.'

'Who did you really leave in charge of the shop?'

'Sohail.'

'Great. You better drop me off home and head back then.'

'You're not coming into work today?'

I could tell he was being half-serious.

'I'm too tired.'

'I thought you slept on flights.'

'Not this time.'

'This must have been really bad. You sure you don't want to talk about it.'

Maybe I *should* have asked Mawlana to pick me up I thought to myself. He would have asked the same, or maybe even less questions as Ranjit. We had reached the lift to go down into the car park, we both stared up at the floor numbers above the door. I decided to move the conversation away.

'Just do me a favour, take the central London route and stop by the garage on the way to Woodford. You know I don't trust Sohail.'

'You underestimate him.'

'Yeah that must be it.'

We made our way to Ranjit's Datsun Sunny and left the car park, before I knew it I was fast asleep.

❋ ❋ ❋

I walked through the front door going over the questions in my mind that Linda was going to ask me later in the day. As I shut it I heard a commotion in the kitchen and then footsteps, I looked up and Linda was drying a mug in her hand.

'What are you doing here?' she asked me.

We both looked at each other perplexed.

'I could you ask you the same thing,' I said to her.

'I'm not the one who's supposed to be a thousand miles away right now. What happened? Why didn't you call? Did your flight get cancelled?'

Great, I was hoping I'd get some respite, but not likely.

'I had a falling out with my mum.'

She stopped drying the mug and put her hands on her hips, a look of concern and confusion on her face.

'So rather than moping around for a few weeks being angry with her I thought I'd just come home,' I continued.

'Salim, you can't just have a row with your mum as soon as you get there and storm off on the first flight back.'

I let out a sigh and made my way to the living room and slumped onto the sofa. I was exhausted and I didn't really want to go through this right now. But I had no choice.

'We all have rows with our parents,' she started up again.

'I didn't just have a row!' I said to her exasperated, trying to keep my voice down. 'She doesn't want me for a son so I did her a favour.'

She sat down next to me and held my hand.

'What happened?'

I shut my eyes for a little bit to regain some composure.

'When I got there, there was a family who had come to see Abbas about getting him married to their daughter. It turns out she told them she had only one son. Him.'

She let go of my hand and put hers on her knees.

'Why did she do that?'

'Because in her mind it was easier for her to not have me than explain to them that I'm not the traditional boy who just does whatever mummy tells them and what society expects of. Their society.'

'Is your mum ashamed of us Salim?'

I had to think about the answer, did she?

'No. She just doesn't want to have to deal with what

people might think.'

'Well what's there to think about? What's wrong with us?'

'You wouldn't understand, it's complicated.'

'Well uncomplicate it.'

'Linda,' I just wanted to give up to just not have to deal with or talk to anyone, but it wasn't going to happen. 'Does your dad accept us?'

She didn't say anything.

'Don't people stare at us when we go outside? Whether it's here in white Woodford or in Asian Whitechapel? At least in Pakistan they have an excuse that theirs is a conservative society. It's not like here where they tell you people can do what they want and everyone just has to accept it. But when you do do something you want they still call you names and stare at you? At least in Pakistan people are practicing the hate they preach.'

'Salim, I understand what you mean. But this is your mum and your family we're talking about, forget about my dad, he and your mum are not the same person. What does our life have anything to do with your brother's?'

'When two people get married, it's not just two people, it's two families that get married.'

'I see. I suppose we're just not good enough for anyone are we?'

She slumped back in the sofa, both our moods were of dejection. I felt sorry for all of us at that moment, and began to wonder what lay ahead of us for our future.

'So why are you at home?' I asked her. I tried to move the conversation away in the hope it would lighten our mood.

She looked down at the floor weighing up what to say. I got nervous, it looked like it was something serious.

'Wasim got suspended.'

'What?!'

'It's alright, it wasn't his fault,' she tried to calm my surprise. 'Another boy was picking on him and he fought back.'

'So if it wasn't his fault why did he get suspended? And why were they picking on him?'

Linda pursed her lips.

'They were picking on him because he's mixed race.'

I got up and started pacing around the room. I was furious, I don't think I've ever been as angry as I was at that moment. I ran my fingers through my hair, I wanted to pull it out, I wanted to scream, I wanted to break everything around me.

'So why was he the one who got suspended?' I asked again.

'I don't know Salim, I don't understand it myself.'

'Where is he now?'

'In his room.'

I made my way out of the room and marched up the stairs.

'Salim what are you doing?'

I didn't answer her, I barged into Wasim's room. He was lying in bed facing away from the door towards the wall, he still had his uniform on.

'Dad?' He shot up.

'Good you still have your uniform on. Put your blazer on, get your bag, you're going back to school.'

'Dad I've been suspended.'

'Salim, what are you doing?' Linda asked behind me.

'I don't give a shit if you've been suspended,' it was the first time he heard me swear. 'You're going back to your *bhan-*

chod school and I'm going to have a word with your bastard of a headmaster.'

'Salim, calm down.'

'No I'm not going to calm down, I'm sick of this shit. Come on Wasim let's go.'

He looked at Linda in desperation unsure of what to do.

'What are you looking at her for? Let's go!'

He got his things together slowly, unsure what any of this was going to lead to. Linda looked on helpless, she didn't know what to say or do. Once he was ready we made our way out of the house into the car and drove to his school in silence.

'Show me the way to your class,' I said to him.

We made our way through the doors and down a long corridor all the classrooms were connected to until we came to a door that said "Year 2 – Mrs Wise". I knocked on the door and opened it without waiting for a response.

Mrs Wise stood in front of us at the head of the class, all of the children were staring.

'Go on Salim, go take your seat.' I told him.

'Uhm Mr Khan,' she was clearly confused. 'Wasim has been suspended.'

'No he hasn't, I'm going to talk to the headmaster right now,' I replied bluntly.

'May I have a word with you outside please?' she asked me as I backed out of the room.

'No you may not,' I managed to say before I shut the door.

I made my way further down the corridor, I hadn't seen the headmaster's office yet so I assumed I just needed to head farther down. I heard a door open behind me which must have been Mrs Wise trying to chase after me. I didn't look back. I reached the main entrance of the school and the reception area.

'I'd like to speak to the headmaster please,' I said to the receptionist curtly.

She looked up from her desk and peered at me over her round glasses, her mouth agape as though I had taken her by surprise.

'Is he expecting you?'

She picked up a sheet of paper which I assumed was the headmaster's schedule for the day.

'No. My son was suspended today and I'd like to discuss it with him.'

'I see. I assume your Wasim's father?'

'Yes.'

'He's already discussed your son's suspension with your wife.'

'Yes I know but I'd like to discuss it with him personally.'

'Um,' she looked over at her colleague unsure of what to say. 'We can see if he's available.'

Just at that moment the headmaster appeared out of his office with a cup in his hand, heading for a coffee break, perfect timing.

'Mr Davids,' I said to him, he looked at me with a sense of reservation. I held out my hand which he embraced back. 'My name is Salim Khan, I'm Wasim's father.'

'Ah Mr Khan, I already discussed your son's suspension with your wife earlier.'

'Yes I'm aware of that, but I just came to let you know that I'm unsuspending him.'

'I beg your pardon?' he said confused.

'I've put him back in class and I'd appreciate it if you suspend the boy who was being racially abusive to him instead.'

'Now see here Mr Khan-'

'No, Mr Davids,' I cut him off. 'I didn't come to this country just so my son could be disparaged for his skin colour.'

He put his cup down in an effort to make himself look more serious.

'Mr Khan, this is unacceptable, I don't know how things work where you come from, but you do not give me orders!'

'That's fine Mr Davids, if you refuse to lift the suspension effective immediately I'll have no choice but to raise a complaint with the board of governors, and also send a letter to the local paper and to the MP, explaining that my son was the victim of racial abuse which you failed to act on, and instead punished him for doing nothing wrong.'

He became flummoxed, unsure of what to say.

'Mr Khan, I can see you've taken this very seriously-'

'My level of seriousness shouldn't make a difference. It's your responsibility to look after these children and you've failed in your duty of care. I shouldn't even have to be here arguing about this in the first place. Now can I assume that you will do the right thing?'

He wasn't used to being talked down to by a parent, let alone a brown one, I must have been the first Asian parent he had had an argument with.

'I'll review the situation with your son Mr Khan, rest assured, I see you feel very strongly about this, and I'm sorry if you're disappointed in my handling of the situation. But I've been a teacher for twenty years, I know what I'm doing and I don't appreciate my efforts being undermined in this way.'

'Well, if you feel you've acted appropriately then you

won't have any issues when you're asked about it by everyone I'm about to send a letter to.'

'Mr Khan,' he held up his hand as if to stop me running him over. 'OK, let's put Wasim back in class and we can review his suspension.'

'And the other boy?'

'Yes, we'll look into disciplinary action against Tom as well.'

'Thank you for your understanding Mr Davids.'

I left the school without saying anything further and made my way back to the car, and for the first time in the last two days, I finally stopped being angry with the world.

CHAPTER 18

Present

I rang the doorbell and waited for the usual lull in response as the ladies in the house scrambled to put their hijabs and niqabs on. Mawlana Ahmed had raised all of his children to be practicing Muslims, but they were left to decide for themselves as to what level they wanted to take their religiosity. One son was a religious scholar, sent to a typical madrassa at a young age, he decided to diversify his studies by attending a "further studies Islamic college" in Cambridge run by an English convert who was both traditionally trained and a lecturer at the university. He came back completely different, a man of letters who could go from discussing obscure medieval texts, to talking about the latest news in global politics, to giving advice to concerned parents about the trouble their children were getting into. Likewise, Mawlana had one daughter who was also a religious student and decided to marry and settle down after finishing her studies. And lastly the third, the youngest was the rebellious one, relatively speaking, she went on to become a doctor.

The door finally opened, it was Qasim, Mawlana's son, he was rocking a baby to sleep in his arms, a white towel hanging over his shoulder.

'Do you want a hand?' I asked him in Urdu.

'Asalaam alaikum Salim uncle, no it's OK,' he said laughing. 'Please come in.'

'It's not a bad time is it?'

It was a rhetorical question, with so many people living in one house it was always a bad time, not that they minded the constant guests they received.

'No of course not, please feel free to go up to the bedroom.'

I took my shoes off and went up the narrow stairs to the one landing, the sound of cooking and children playing was muffled by the kitchen door. Upstairs on the landing four doors surrounded me, I knocked on the one immediately in front.

'Huh? What is it? Why are you knocking?' came the weak voice from inside.

'It's me,' I said to him in Punjabi. 'Can I come in?'

'*Haan haan*, why are you being so formal for?'

I walked in and Mawlana Ahmed was swinging himself out of bed to sit up.

'Please stay lying down,' I urged him raising my hand.

'Don't be silly,' he said. 'I need an excuse to get out of bed. Not that I am getting out of bed, but just sitting up in it,' he wasn't quite sure what he was trying to say. 'Whatever.'

I sat down in the chair next to him, where everyone who came to him for advice or just a silly chitchat came to sit. His paunch had grown bigger the last few years, his diabetes and old age had become debilitating. Gone were the days when he would perform two shifts in a factory back to back in a single day and never miss a prayer. Now he struggled to move around the house, let alone leave it. His face was sagged and his eyes dark, his familiar turban sat on the bedside, in its normal place was a shining bald patch. He still wore a white shalwar kameez all the time, which matched with his long white beard.

'The one thing I regret most Salim,' he started to say without any prelude. 'Was I didn't ask Allah for a quick death.'

'Don't say things like that Mawlana saab.'

'It's true,' he responded, raising his voice slightly. 'This is no life Salim, lying in bed all day, being a burden on my family. My children should be looking after their children, not their parents.'

Decorum wanted me to argue with him in a friendly way, to lighten his mood, but I didn't have it in me today. I begrudgingly admitted to myself he had a bit of a point.

'But we must be content with what Allah decides for us. This is what I get for my sins.'

'If that's the case for you there's no hope for the rest of us Mawlana saab.'

'Hmph, everyone has their sins Salim. It's best Allah punishes you in this world for them, the other option is to be punished for them in the next. And that's something I wish for no one.'

He looked at me steely, his deep eyes pulled me in, they hadn't changed since his younger days. Many people had told me they had felt awe struck when he looked at them straight in the eyes, I knew exactly what they meant. Even Ranjit would say it, he once told me in a different time he would have become Muslim just by looking into Mawlana's eyes.

'What brings you to see an old man?' he asked.

'I bring sad news Mawlana. My mother has passed away.'

'Hmm,' he said nodding. 'I know.'

'How?' I asked in bewilderment.

'I had a dream.'

If it weren't for Mawlana's little miracles here and there I don't know what would have happened to the little religion I had left.

'What did you see?' I asked him.

'I saw the fields outside your family's home-'

'And me standing at her grave.'

'Hmm,' he nodded.

'What else?'

'Nothing, that was all.'

'Why didn't you call me, or say anything?'

'I didn't know if it was a true dream, or just my imagination. I didn't want to worry you,' he coughed into a tissue raspily, trying to catch his breath. 'If it were true I was sure you would come to see me eventually.'

'What do you think I should do?'

He looked at me, his eyes tired but yet still full of strength in meaning and insight.

'I think you already know what you need to do.'

'Go back.'

'Hmm,' he nodded in agreement.

'I want to, but what will that achieve?'

'Achieve? There is nothing to achieve,' he swung his legs round again and lay back stretching his legs out in front resting his head against the headboard, he was tired from sitting and couldn't hold himself up any longer. He stared into the space in front of him. 'If you don't go back to visit your mother's grave at least once, you will regret it.'

'But it's not like I can make amends with her.'

'I advised you many years ago to make amends with her Salim,' he raised his voice slightly admonishing me like he usually did. 'Forgive her her mistakes, have mercy as Allah has mercy. But alas, man was created weak, whether it be in body, like me, or in emotion, like you, with your inability to overcome your anger.'

His words struck me to my core. Would I swap places with him right now if I could? Suffer from a weakness of the body, rather than a weakness of character, just so I wouldn't have this cloud of regret hanging over me now? Maybe. He once told me never to think about what could have been or what could have not been, but to live in the moment, and take what God gives you, but never be hesitant to make up for the mistakes of your past.

'We will all be taken to account for our mistakes Salim,' his voice slowing down. 'You, your mother, me, all of us. Did we try our best to make amends with those we love before our time was over?'

It was as if he had read my mind and wanted to hammer the point home.

'Your mother's pen has now been lifted. What will you do while yours is still writing?'

He started to breath heavily, letting out an occasional cough.

'She made a mistake Salim,' he continued. 'Forgive her while you are still alive.' He repeated himself. 'Go back to your home, your first home, your *real* home. Imagine as if she is still alive and you are making a journey to forgive her. You have been away for far too long. You stayed away because you were angry, going back now will be the end of this sad chapter of your life.'

I said nothing, I reflected on his words as I too stared into space. He turned to look at me.

'What's wrong?' he asked.

'Nothing. I was already thinking of going back but I

wasn't sure why. You make some good points as usual Mawlana but I feel like it's too late, making amends with someone after they have passed away? It's an empty gesture.'

'Salim, we believe in life after death, forgiving someone whether in this world or the next, is the same. But even, just for argument's sake, we did not believe that, do you not need this closure in your life? How did you find out she died?'

'I received a letter.'

'Who from?'

It was as if he already knew.

'I, don't know. I called Abbas and he said it wasn't him.'

'Hmm, so your mother is the only one who could have sent it. She knew her time was coming. She wrote to you so you would know, she *wanted* you to know. There is no doubt about it, she is waiting for you, you must go back.

Hmm, our old village, I miss it a lot you know Salim? I wish I could go back there, to my parent's house, live out my last few remaining days there where I was born. Not to be surrounded by the sound of traffic, but the sound of the fields, the animals, the call to prayer. Even if they all do sound like donkeys competing with each other.'

We both laughed and it lightened the mood a little.

'Do you remember it Salim? Don't you miss it? We have been in this country longer than we were in Pakistan. But yet, such nostalgia, such memories we have for the place. Because that is where we were born, that is where our mothers raised us. That's why we still call it home. I wish I could visit my parent's graves and recite Fatiha for them one last time.'

The brief lull in sombreness was over. Mawlana's eyes were watery.

'You must go back Salim. If not for yourself, then for the

both of us. Visit her grave, and visit my parent's graves as well. See your brother, make amends with him as well, he did nothing wrong, do not cut off ties with him just because you were upset with your mother.'

As he was talking his voice slowly faded into snoring and he fell asleep. I looked at him, I didn't feel sorry for him, but in that moment seeing him helpless like a child, I truly felt like I loved him. He and Munny were the two people in my life who would replace the gap left by my father. Munny had died a few years after my last visit to Pakistan. His son had called me, he eventually made it back from Afghanistan, and his father told him to call me if he died. I was bereft for so long I don't remember how long it was until I returned back to normal. And now it seemed Mawlana's time was also soon to be at an end as well. My one mother was gone, and now all of the men I considered to be a father to me would be gone soon.

I sat there in silence looking at him snoring away for a long time. Hoping he might wake up and not realise he had fallen asleep. But it didn't look like it was going to happen.

I embraced his hand gently so as not to wake him and then got up to leave slowly closing the door behind me. Downstairs the kids were still causing a commotion behind closed doors. I let myself out.

Outside, the garden was starting to become overgrown and some of the plants were slowly starting to die. A sign that Mawlana hadn't had a chance to tend to it for a while, gardening was the one pastime he had.

I got in the car and just sat there. I looked at the house and slightly regretted leaving him there like that, I wanted to go back inside and just sit with him again, even if it was just to watch him sleep. There was a calmness in just being with him, and now it was gone and my heart was turbulent again. But I just sat there, wondering what life would be like with Mawlana gone.

CHAPTER 19

1998

"Pandemonium earlier today at the Macpherson Inquiry in Elephant and Castle where the suspects of the racist murder of Stephen Lawrence made an appearance. An angry group of demonstrators barged into the inquiry where there were scuffles as one officer was punched on the chin, and an attempt was made to attack one of the suspects. Afterwards as they left they were pelted with projectiles as police had to hold the crowd back. It's been 5 years since the A-Level student was brutally stabbed to death waiting for a bus simply because of the colour of his skin, and the protestors were demanding justice and that the police be taken to account for their failings in the case."

'Did Wasim say anything about going to this protest?' Linda asked.

I looked up from my newspaper at her, which was running the same story. I had only been half listening.

'No, did he say anything to you?'

'No, that's why I'm asking.'

'Well if he didn't tell you anything he definitely wouldn't have told me. It's not like he has a PhD to finish or anything.'

It was the late afternoon in July and as the sun was starting to lower in the sky as it filled the living room with light. Linda was watching the six o'clock news while trying out crocheting, another new hobby in the list of hobbies she had been attempting recently.

'Oh God, I hope he's alright,' Linda looked solemnly at her little project.

'I'm sure he'll be fine. He's an expert at these things.'

'He's meant to becoming an expert in law, not being an angry student the rest of his life.'

'What do you expect from someone who decided to do their thesis on Police Brutality and Institutionalised Racism?'

I always had to say the word "institutionalised" slowly, too many syllables for my liking.

'Not just the first person from my family to go to university but do a PhD as well. I just wish sometimes he would have done something a little more, I don't know, less controversial.'

I chuckled and looked at her.

'You're getting soft in your old age. What happened to the young radical working-class leftist who married an immigrant and took her young son to anti-racist protests?'

'Oh don't be so dramatic. And if I remember correctly you were the one went to that protest and almost got killed at the end of it.'

'I did *not* almost get killed, and that's not the only one I'm talking about. There was the one for the Falklands, and then there was Iraq, apartheid.'

'Oh yeah.'

'Oh yeah,' I mimicked her. 'You can't raise a son like ours and not expect him to turn out the way he did.'

'Uh excuse me,' she put down her project and looked at me. 'Don't put all this blame on me.'

'I didn't blame you for anything, I'm not the one complaining about him attending protests or doing this PhD of his.'

'Hmm,' was her only response.

She went back to her crochet.

A key turned in the front door and the latch unlocked.

'Speak of the devil,' said Linda.

Wasim stomped through the hallway and made his way up the stairs without saying anything.

'Good evening Mr Khan,' Linda shouted after him. 'If you have a moment can you come here please.'

Wasim walked into the living room looking at her expectantly. He was wearing a t-shirt and jeans and his hair was a mess.

'Where have you been?'

'At uni where else?'

'You didn't go anywhere else today?'

He looked at me, I glanced up at him and went back to the newspaper.

'Maybe, why do you ask?'

'Where did you go?'

'Met up with some friends.'

'Friends from Elephant and Castle?' I asked him.

He rolled his eyes and sighed.

'Yes I went to the protest.'

'Did you hurt any police officers?' I asked him.

'No.'

'Did you launch projectiles at the suspects?'

'Well yeah everyone did.'

Linda put her crochet down and looked at him solemnly.

'Was, whatever happened to *peaceful* protest?' Linda asked him.

'Yeah well you know, murder someone in cold blood you get a coffee in the face.'

'Wasim! That is not the attitude to have.'

'Everyone was angry at those cocky pricks, what did you expect people to do?'

'We understand Was. We understand people are angry, the stuff that people like us have to had to go through, we know what racism is. But come on, that isn't the solution.'

'Yeah but here you are sitting around, watching TV and reading a newspaper.'

'Wasim,' I inadvertently raised my voice slightly. 'You don't get to lecture me about racism, thank you.'

'I didn't mean it like that dad. You weren't there, you would have done the same thing if you had seen those guys.'

'Wasim, do you really want to risk getting arrested for some silly misdemeanour?' I continued. 'Have you thought about what would happen to your future, your PhD if you got arrested over something silly like this?' I pointed to the TV. 'Doesn't this whole case show you what happens if you give the police an inch? Just like they left that young man to die and not bother to do anything to convict his killers, they'd be more than happy to stick you in jail for any little thing.'

I felt it was a half-truth, the police were no longer as bad as they used to be. When we were in Whitechapel all those years ago they simply did not care about us, things were slowly starting to change, and this whole situation with Stephen Lawrence and the pressure his family was putting on felt like it was about time the inadequacies of the police came to the fore.

'We're not telling you not to protest,' putting my voice back to normal. 'God knows there's no stopping you. Just be sensible.'

'Alright fine,' he held up his hands. 'I get it, I'll be more *sensible* going forward. But can you please stop lecturing me like a child.'

'We're not lecturing you,' I explained to him. 'We're looking out for you. And plus if you don't get your thesis finished you'll never finally get married and move out.'

Linda let out a chuckle.

'If your grandfather could see you,' Linda said. '"A working man has gotta earn a living by his hands" he would say,' she imitated a gruff cockney accent. 'God rest his soul.'

'I thought you hated him,' Wasim said as he sat down watching the protest on the TV, probably looking for himself.

'Don't say that,' I said to him quietly.

'No he's right. I did hate my father, because he hated yours for no reason.' She let out a long sigh. 'But he was still my dad.'

There was now a sombreness in the room. Between Linda talking about her father, and the things being shown on the TV, how far had things really come along?

'Speaking of parents,' I turned to Wasim. 'Mawlana Ahmed came back from Pakistan yesterday, your grandmother sent you a shalwar kameez.'

'What am I going to do with it?' he asked nonchalantly.

'Wear it for Eid, wear it to a wedding, wear it around the house while it's hot. Whatever you want.'

'How did she even know my size?'

'I don't know, she must have guessed. Just try it on and see.'

'Why don't you take it back to her, make amends with her, and then give her my actual size and make sure that it fits.'

I was annoyed he used my fraught relationship with Ami as a butt of a joke. I ignored him and tried to pretend I was reading my newspaper.

'Come on dad, you can't continue having this relationship with Dadi through proxies.'

'When your Dadi is willing to apologise I'll be waiting.'

'What is with Asians and never-ending grudges?'

'What do you mean?' I asked him.

'All of my Asian friends have ongoing family feuds. Disputes over land back home, or inheritance from a dead relative. Ahmed's mum hasn't spoken to his aunt for fifteen years just because of some silly wedding game, something about giving the groom milk to drink or something.'

'Yeah, the bride's sisters offer to give the groom milk to drink in exchange for money. They did it at Piya's wedding remember?'

Piya was Ranjit's daughter, she had gotten married the summer before.

'Oh yeah, I think I was confused about it then as well. But anyway, apparently Ahmed's mum used sour milk at her sister's wedding and he ended up spitting it out on the stage.'

'Hah! That's brilliant.'

'Yeah sure,' Wasim didn't seem to think so. 'That one prank cost them fifteen years of never talking to each other.'

'Well maybe she should learn to lighten up.'

'Yeah, just like how you should learn to forgive Dadi.'

'Hmm.'

He had gotten me into a corner I couldn't back out of.

'Wasim is right Salim. Your mum is not like my dad, it was nearly fifteen years ago. Abbas has gotten married and had kids, it's all just water under the bridge now.'

'When she wants to call me and talk I'll be ready.'

Wasim and Linda looked at each other but didn't say anything. They both used to say I was stubborner than a mule. I suppose they were right, ironically I was too stubborn to admit it.

* * *

I don't know how long I was staring at the list of telephone numbers for Pakistan in my little diary. I was sitting in the attic with the desk lamp providing the only light shining down at the worn little leather book.

I didn't understand why I was being so hesitant. Was it because I didn't want to talk to her? No that wasn't it, otherwise I wouldn't be sitting here right now. Was I afraid she wouldn't want to speak to me? Maybe. Was it just the sheer nervousness of speaking to her after so long? It must have been all of those things together.

I decided I'd had enough, I was diving in, I picked up the receiver on the phone without thinking and dialled the number. The international dialling tone started to ring and I waited. It kept ringing but no answer. I was getting ready to hang up.

'Hello?'

Was that Ami? Her voice sounded tired and had a hint of anxiousness.

'Ami?'

Silence for a moment.

'Salim?'

'Yes Ami it's me how are you?'

'*Haan*, just fine. Is everything OK?'

'Yes I just thought I'd give you a call to see how you are.'

'Oh, OK,' she said surprised. 'You called so late I thought maybe there was an emergency or something.'

Late? I looked at the digital clock on the desk, it said 21:04. Shit. They were four hours ahead, in my anxious state I had completely forgotten.

'*Arre yaar*, I'm sorry Ami I forgot that you're ahead of us.'

She let out a short laugh, it felt good to hear her laughter after so many years, and I felt less guilty for waking her now that I knew she wasn't upset.

'It's fine I wasn't sleeping anyway.'

I was pretty sure she was lying. I wanted to ask her what she was doing, but I decided against it in case she was actually sleeping and would have to make something up.

'So what made you remember your mother at this time of night?'

'Oh, Mawlana sahib gave us the clothes you sent I wanted to thank you for them.'

'It's not a problem. Mawlana showed me a photo from your friend's daughter's wedding, Ranjit is it? So I had to guess Wasim's size from that.'

I had no idea Mawlana was keeping her up to date on everything. But it didn't surprise me.

'How is your wife, Linda?'

'She's fine, these days she's started taking up, I don't know what it's called in Urdu or Punjabi, but it's called crocheting, it's like knitting.'

'Yes, I know it, they call it crocheting everywhere.'

'Yeah, the whole house is fall of all of her little creations.'

She chortled.

'How are things with you?'

'Oh fine, looking after Abbas's children with his wife. What else could a grandmother ask for? *Alhumdulilah*. Zubair is starting university soon.'

Abbas's eldest, I knew because Mawlana also kept us abreast of them as well.

'That's good.'

'Listen Salim, it's good to talk after so long but it's quite late.'

'Of course, I'm sorry. I'll call back another time.'

'OK Salim, take care of yourself, give my salaam to your family.'

'Of course, give my salaam to everyone. *Khudahafiz*.'

'*Khudahafiz*.'

I placed the receiver down not knowing what to think. It was such a brief conversation the awkwardness of which only started to sink in after it had ended. Did she really want to talk to me? Was she just being polite? Or was I just overthinking it? The brevity of the call felt like there was a coldness between us, just a formality, with only a hint of familiarity.

I said to myself I would call her back, or thought maybe she would call me. But it didn't happen. The slight awakening of our relationship, the late night conversation, felt like waking up from a deep sleep in the middle of night, only to fall back asleep again, half- remembering you had even woken up.

CHAPTER 20

2002

'I just got the call from the Met, they managed to convince a judge to extend his detention, now he could be in for a week.'

'Great,' Wasim muttered down the phone sarcastically as he scattered papers around his desk. 'Any idea if they have anything on him yet?'

'Doesn't sound like it. This is going to be another head banging against the wall jobby.'

Another one of Michael's weird analogies for describing a case.

'Poor guy's stressed out.'

'Wouldn't anyone be?'

'Yeah I suppose. The questions they were asking him today, honestly, "If you could fight in Bosnia or Afghanistan which would you choose?".'

Wasim sat back in his chair confused.

'Why would they ask a question like that? How does that help them with their investigation?'

'They're clutching at straws mate. Trying to get him to

slip up and say something stupid.'

'Please tell me you put that out right away.'

'Come on what do you take me for? Of course I did.'

'So their investigation is based on what? Run it by me again.'

'Calls to a house in Karachi which the ISI have claimed has been used for terrorism, our guy claims it's a shared house and he was calling a relative. A bunch of web searches that they're keeping classified, my guess is it's GCHQ handiwork with no warrant, obviously won't hold up in court. And some pictures of him with an assault rifle in Pakistan, he claims he went hunting.'

'What do you make of it.'

'I mean, not gonna lie, he *could* be a terrorist with all that on him, I can see where the Met are coming from, but my gut tells me he's just unlucky. Remember that seminar you did on Muslim groups for the company? He's a TJ.'

'Tablighi Jamat.'

'Yeah that's it. He's docile, quiet, shy. Not terrorist material. He looked proper out of place in the photo with the rifle, it was bigger than he was. He doesn't have the usual macho bullshit online that we see the guilty guys having.'

'Hmm. Still sounds like it'll go to court.'

'Yeah, that's what I'm thinking.'

'Alright well, tomorrow's a new day.'

'Yeah right. You still at the office?'

'Sixteen hours.'

'Glamourous life of high flying lawyer eh? You turning in or sleeping at the office?'

'One email left.'

'Yeah right, until you get the next one. Speak to you in the morning.'

'Yeah see you mate.'

Wasim hung up the phone. He was exhausted, the mix of office lights and a bright computer screen dried his eyes out. He would take a break every now and again to stare out of the window into the darkness of the night, but when turning back to the jarring light of his screen his eyes didn't feel any better.

He rolled his chair around and stared out of the office window again down onto the grimy streets of East London below. He remembered this spot from his childhood, it used to be a factory, now it was a shiny office block on the edges of Whitechapel and Aldgate looking down onto the graffitied walls and hip young white people slowly moving into the area. How things had changed so quickly. He and his family moved away from here to escape the racism and the crime. Now they had walking tours to show you all of Banksy's latest pieces.

In that small time after the Stephen Lawrence inquiry it felt like things were starting to get better, things were changing, racism was on the way out. The new century brought with it a new era for minorities in Britain. It all came crashing down with those towers in 2001. Now every day it seemed like there was always something about Muslims in the news. The only time he remembered the media making a furore about Islam was the Salman Rushdie affair years ago, after that died down no one cared anymore.

Wasim felt it was ironic, or was it destiny? That he decided on pursuing a career in law rather than sticking with academia right when it was the busiest time to become a lawyer who was also Muslim. It seemed with each new piece the media put out, more police operations lead to more cases the firm had to deal with. And as they were largely legal aid funded human rights specialists, there was plenty of work to go around. A raid on a house, an unlawful stop and search, charges of terrorism, they varied in their nature, and the pieces of at least 80 of those cases were scattered around Wasim's desk.

He swivelled back round on his chair to his computer. One last email. A detective at Barkingside station was meant to provide a report on a complaint raised about a raid on a business. The police claimed a warehouse was being used to make bombs. Turns out they were mixing perfumes, the cheap roller ones they sold in Islamic shops a dime a dozen all over East London. They confiscated the wares, confirmed it wasn't going to blow anything up, but hadn't handed it back.

Wasim took a deep sigh. Is this what his PhD was really for? Chasing up cheap perfumes? No, it was the principal. Wasim's job was to uphold people's rights, the rights his parents had fought for. The fight they put in him because of everything they had had to deal with.

Wasim rattled a quick email on his keyboard and sent it. He would have to chase it up anyway so no need to write anything substantial now, it would come in the follow up. He put on his blazer, picked up his phone and wallet, turned the light off and walked out of his office before anything else came through.

He had a quick look around to see if anyone was also still working. No one, he was the last to leave today, it wasn't always the case.

As it was a weeknight the streets were relatively quiet, not many revellers making their way to Shoreditch or having a curry before a night drinking. As he approached Paradise Fried Chicken, his favourite chicken shop, he thought he should really try to cut back on the stuff. But then what was he going to eat when he got home?

He gave his salaam to the owner who had been in the area almost as long as his dad had been. Ate his burger and chips in a hurry and then took the central line to Snaresbrook where he had bought a flat that he hardly lived in.

As the central line chugged along he went through his messages, one from Nasima, his girlfriend who he was taking his time proposing to, and a couple of missed calls from dad. Not like dad to call, it was usually mum who did.

He waited until the train came out of the tunnel at Leyton and then dialled. Salim picked up after a couple of rings.

'Asalaam alaikum,' Salim greeted him almost sombrely.

'Walaikum salaam. How's it going dad?'

'Oh fine, *alhumdulilah*.'

Wasim could tell something was up.

'I saw you called me a couple of times is everything OK?'

'Oh yeah fine, same old you know,' he laughed.

He was being the typical Pakistani dad hiding his emotions. A bit more so than usual.

'What's wrong dad?'

Salim paused for a moment.

'A couple of guys came into the garage today, said some stupid things and then threw some stuff around, tried to take the money out of the till, made a total mess of the place.'

'Is everyone OK?'

'Yeah, everyone is fine, just a little shook up. You can't expect to cause too much trouble in place with so many heavy tools lying around.'

He forced out a little snicker, but they both knew it wasn't funny.

'Why did they do that? Were they disgruntled customers or what?'

'They were calling us terrorists and talking about 9/11. I don't know. Basically because we're Muslim they decided to cause trouble. That's why I wanted to call you, make sure everything is OK, and you know, hoping no one is causing problems with you.'

'Come on dad, it's not like it was a coordinated thing against us.'

'Yeah I know, but since you moved out we haven't been talking as much as we used to, so I just wanted to make sure you were safe is all.'

It was strange feeling sorry for your father. The feeling of listening to someone who held your hand for so many years now sounding helpless. He looked up and saw the train was pulling into Woodford station.

'I'm coming over dad.'

'No Wasim it's OK, I just wanted to check up on you.'

'I'm almost there already. Put a roti on for me.'

He hung up the phone before Salim had a chance to persist. Wasim wasn't hungry after his full meal at the chicken shop but he hoped having Salim cook something would lighten his mood a bit.

※ ※ ※

The familiar smell of salan (they never used the word curry) permeated the house as Wasim walked in. He found Salim in the kitchen spinning a roti on the tawa, memories of seeing his father in the kitchen cooking Pakistani cuisine flooded his mind. Salim had similar memories of Ranjit doing the same when he was Wasim's age some forty years earlier.

'Just one please.'

Salim was caught surprised.

'Asalaam alaikum, I didn't hear you come in.'

He went back to the roti as Wasim put his bag down and placed his blazer on the back of one of the dining chairs.

'Where's mum?'

'Asleep.'

'Bit early isn't it?'

'It's 11 o'clock Wasim.'

'What…?'

He looked up at the kitchen clock which had just gone past 11.

'Damn, I hadn't even realised. Why didn't you say anything when I called?'

'I did!' he let out a laugh. 'But you hung up on me so quickly.'

'Oh I'm so sorry.'

'It's fine I hadn't eaten anyway and I was starting to feel hungry too.'

Salim would always eat when he got home. The fact he hadn't eaten yet meant he really was shook up by what had happened at the garage. It wasn't like him to lose his appetite.

'What salan is it?'

'Chicken.'

Great, more chicken he thought to himself.

The rest of the night was spent with the two eating dinner and talking idly. Wasim knew he was father was the typical Asian dad who struggled to talk about his feelings, a lot of that had rubbed off on him as well, so he tried empathising with him the way he would feel most comfortable, by just talking about normal everyday stuff to make it feel like it was an average day.

Wasim ate more than he thought he would. The tantalizing mix of lots of ginger, chilli and tomato, that was so characteristic of Salim's cooking, was too good to resist. It had been a while since he had eaten it. He could have easily eaten a second roti.

Eventually he had to address the elephant in the room.

'How much has the garage been damaged dad?'

'Oh, not much. Just some broken glass and stuff chucked around. Someone's coming tomorrow to fix the windows. We'll be open as usual.'

He said it all rather nonchalantly.

'You sure you want to go back and not take a few days off?'

'Come on Wasim. I've had to deal with worse in my time.'

'Have you?'

Wasim never remembered hearing about his father having to deal with overt racism before, but he was sure he must have faced it.

'Oh yeah. Back in the old days there were parts of London I wouldn't go to. Bethnal Green used to be racist central.'

'Really?'

Walking through Bethnal Green today you wouldn't have thought it.

'Oh yeah. Whitechapel was where all the Asians, mostly Bengalis were, and Bethnal Green was mostly whites up until a few years before we moved away from there. You probably don't remember how bad it used to be back then.'

Wasim faced a fair bit of racism in his school in Woodford, never really in Whitechapel, where there was sizeable Asian population of kids, and the white children were all far too young to be racist. But as he grew up in Woodford, which at the time was still predominately white, he had faced his fair share of irregular problems. He never really talked about it with his parents. There was just the one time he remembered his form tutor didn't take his complaints seriously, but after Salim stormed into the headmaster's office, well that was the end of that. Woodford was a largely middle-class area, so there wasn't much racism even at that time, but it did exist. Now thinking about those experiences he wondered what his father must have had to go through on a daily basis just to eke out a living. What both his parents must have had to go through as a mixed couple, when mixed couples were rare. It was at that moment Wasim realised how lucky he was to have been born in the time and era that he was, and to have parents who must have had to go through so much for him to get to where he was now.

'Before this 9/11 thing happened,' Salim continued. 'I thought the chapter on racism was done in this country, but I guess I was wrong.'

'Yeah, I know what you mean. Can't imagine what I would have been doing if it had never happened. Seems like the police are constantly after anyone with a beard.'

'Yeah…'

They sat in silence, father and son, looking back on the past, not knowing what the future held.

CHAPTER 21

Present

I slumped down into my seat on the plane finally. I hadn't flown on a plane for a very long time, the last flight I took was well before 9/11. All of these new procedures and protocols made everything feel so drawn out. I twisted the vent above and felt the cold air cool the sweat on my forehead. Getting through the airport, going through security, finding the gate, going through security again, walking through the tight aisle on the plane, all of it was a bit much in this old age of mine.

I looked to my right and someone had already laid his head back, snoring away with his mouth open. I secretly envied him. To the left an old lady was hobbling down the aisle stopping at each row to check if it was hers, causing a holdup of impatient passengers behind her. From further back I heard someone remonstrating with another passenger about stuffing a bag into an already full compartment.

Despite the changes to protocol, Pakistani passengers hadn't changed much it would seem.

I took out some of the photos I had found the last few days from my coat pocket, and began to go over them lazily, reliving each memory again and again, unsure of what I was trying to achieve. Maybe if I looked back on better days it would lift the sadness I was going through. But through all of the memories there was always the lingering shadow of my relationship with Ami. My mind began to wonder about things that could have been. Could I have brought Ami to live in England? What would that have been like? To have her here with me for so many years, to have her see Wasim grow up. All the "could haves" and "would haves" just lingered on my mind when I already had so much to go through.

'Asalaam Alaikum,' an elderly lady greeted me as she sat down in the vacant seat next to me.

'Walaikum salaam,' I murmured back, she took me by surprise almost as I was lost in my thoughts.

She wore a white shalwar kameez with a golden dupatta wrapped loosely around her head. Her complexion had a youthfulness to it, the only indication that she was around the same age as me were her thick glasses and light wrinkles around her eyes.

I put my photos back into my pocket.

'You're going back after a long time aren't you?' she asked me in Urdu.

'Excuse me?'

'You're going back to Pakistan after a long time aren't you? I saw you looking at your photos. You're anxious I can tell.'

I smiled.

'It's only been forty years.'

'Forty years! Why so long? You don't have family there anymore?'

'I do, my brother is still there. But my mother passed away last week, that's why I'm going now.'

She muttered the prayer said when someone passes away under her breath.

'I'm so sorry to hear that, may God forgive her. I can imagine it's quite a difficult time for you, especially having been away so long. I hope God makes it easy for you and your family.'

'*Ameen.*'

'I hope you don't mind me asking, and I hope I don't offend you, but did you never wish to go see your mother after all these years?'

Her question dug into me like a sharp knife, especially as she asked me such a personal question after only having just met me.

'I did, but, it's complicated. You see I married an English woman, which as you can imagine for someone to do at that time when we were young, was almost unheard of. And it never sat well with her. So it caused a souring of our relationship.'

The lady smiled wryly.

'Brother, I've been a mother for longer than you've been away from Pakistan. Trust me, the dearest things to a woman are her children. No matter how mad she gets at them, no matter what they do, she will always be the one who gave birth to them, raised them, looked after them. A true mother would never abandon her children. Whether physically or spiritually. Everything a mother does is because she thinks she knows best for her children, even if she is wrong, at least her intention was in the right place.'

I reflected on her words as the plane began to back away from the gate and the engines started to whirr.

'Maybe you're right. I've been thinking about it a lot recently, maybe my mother isn't the reason I've been away so long. Maybe it's me. I didn't go back, because maybe I didn't want to.'

'Why is that?'

'After I told my mother I was going to marry Linda, my wife, it felt like I had lost a part of her, she seemed so upset, every time I would talk to her on the phone it would seem that way. She was my main connection to Pakistan, and so I came to see that link with a hint of sadness. Now I see all these people around me,' I motioned to all the people sitting around us, the Pakistanis. 'And I feel like a stranger. I feel like I've forgotten who I am and where I came from.'

'You don't have any Asian friends?'

'I do. But I don't see them as much as when I was younger, I spend more time with my family. But when I do meet them, they're all like me, we've been here since the 60s and 70s, we all hate to admit it, but we have lost a part of ourselves from being away from where we came from for so long.'

'You're speaking Urdu with me aren't you? So you certainly remember your tongue. You're going back to see your family, and to remember your mother, so you haven't forgotten them, and they are the roots from which you came from. Just because you have left a place for a long time, it doesn't mean you forget it. Even if you stay in a place for a short while, like a traveller stopping on a path, you will form a bond with that place forever. It may be that you did something as mundane as have a tea or a coffee there, but as long as that memory is there that place will always stay with you. Then what about your family, which you can never forget? The place you were born, where you spent your childhood. Because you can never forget the people and places you left behind, you will never forget who you are and where you have come from. You don't have to belong to one place your whole life. People have moved from place to place throughout human history. You can be English and Pakistani at the same time, and so can your children. Life is not like one of those silly questions on the form English people ask you to fill in, are you "British Asian", "British Pakistani", it's all *bakwaas*, nonsense. All that matters is how you feel, be what makes you comfortable brother. Trust me, you have not forgotten who you are. I know a Pakistani when I see one!'

She finished off with a short laugh and I smiled back. She turned away to look out the window to see the plane approach the runway. I took the photos back out of my pocket and stared at the first one, a faded black and white image of me as an infant being held by a young Ami in the courtyard of our home. The plane began to speed up as it charged down the runway for take-off, a heavy rain began to fall and caused the drops on the window to be louder than they otherwise would.

'You're right,' I said to her. She turned her head back to me. 'I may not feel like I'm the same person who left Pakistan, but I certainly remember him, that boy. I don't think I could ever forget him. He may have changed, but he certainly can't forget where he came from.'

'I think all you need to do brother, is remember. Let the old you into himself. Soon you will lose all this anxiety within you. The English say for people who pass away "May they rest in peace", I say, those who have passed away, such as your mother, are already at peace. It's their loved ones left behind who need to find "peace". Remember your old self, and you will find peace. *Inshallah.*'

※ ※ ※

The heat was unbearable, and being in the uncomfortable and dusty old bus, amongst all the other people didn't make it any better. I began to miss Munny and I thought about him and how he would always take me to and from the airport.

Although everything in the bus seemed familiar, everything outside of it wasn't. Shops lined the entire road when before there would be nothing for miles at a time. Traffic constantly streamed in both directions, constantly blaring their long excessive horns, the bus swerving dangerously wide every now and again to overtake a slow-moving bullock cart or a cyclist. In the past I could stare out of the window and lose my thoughts in the fields beyond, now it was impossible, the constant moving to and fro left no room to think.

'You coming from abroad?' asked the man next to me in gruff Punjabi. He had the look of a labourer, skinny, dishevelled, dark skin, stubble, wearing a stained light blue shalwar kameez. I realised I was the only one on the bus not wearing shalwar kameez and it made me stand out.

'Yeah.'

'Where from? Dubai?'

'England.'

'*Aha*,' his gleeful smile exposed his pan stained teeth. 'Very good, very good. How come you're taking the bus? No driver?'

'No.'

'Where are you going? My stop is the one after this one, my brother-in-law can you take you.'

'It's OK, the next village is my stop.'

'OK.'

He turned away but I knew what was coming next.

'Brother, you wouldn't be able to spare some money would you? I don't get paid that much and my mother needs medicine. You wouldn't be able to help at all would you?'

The Radio Pakistan billboard came into view signalling we were arriving at the village, the ad was the same one I remembered, but it had yellowed and tattered, years of billposters infringed on it from all sides. As the bus slowed down and manoeuvred its way off the road onto the dirt track to let people off, I got up to make my way to the front.

'Please whatever you can spare,' the labourer placed his hand on Salim's arm. 'I wouldn't normally ask but you seem like a good honest man.'

I reached into my pocket and took out the first note that came into my reach and gave it to him. He didn't even bother to see how much it was, but I knew I didn't have any small notes.

'Please brother if you could spare some more I would be so grateful.'

Normally I would have been disgruntled at his audacity after I was sure I gave him quite a lot, but not today, today I didn't care. I ignored him and got off the bus with a few other passengers. The sunlight was oppressive as it bore down on me, the other people getting off didn't seem phased. I looked up at the roof of the bus to make eye contact with one of the young men riding in "economy class" and gestured towards my suitcase which he brought down for me. I looked at the young boy's eyes, he looked about the same age I was when I first left Pakistan, wearing a cheaply made faded red chequered shirt and jeans.

'How old are you?'

'Eighteen sir.'

'You study?'

'No sir,' he said smirking. 'I don't have time for studies, I have seven brothers and sisters and I'm the oldest.'

'So what do you do for a living?'

'Anything I can get my hands on. Yesterday I was in a restaurant, day before that I was serving tea in an office.'

I wondered what it might have been like if time was rewound and I had decided never to leave. What would it have been like? Would I be in any different a position from this young man? While I laboured in a factory in England, this young man did so here.

I reached into my pocket full of notes and took out whatever came first.

'It's OK uncle,' the young man gently placing his hand on mine. 'I got paid well the last two days. It's fine. Allah has provided for me.'

He bobbed his head with a wide beaming smile.

'Take it,' I insisted. 'Use it for your family.'

'It's OK, really. I hope you don't mind me saying, but you look like something has happened in your life recently, I wouldn't feel right taking your money from you. Please keep it.'

The young man turned around and climbed back up onto the roof. All the other passengers who had disembarked had by now scattered away. The bus gave a creak and a groan and it was off, leaving a trail of exhaust fumes behind. I stood there on the edge of the dirt path and watched the bus and the young man on top of it leave. There was a chai stall at the other side of the road, the men stared grimacing, wondering why I was stood there watching the bus drive away.

As it faded into the distance I extended the handle on the suitcase and began to roll it behind me on a path that I used to feel was like a part of me. Now it felt like reliving a dream, it seemed familiar, and not at the same time. The turns and bends were all the same, but where there used to be a home was now an empty plot of weeds and sand, and where there used to be nothing, there was now a ramshackle home built. I tried to recall if it ever felt this hot to me, and whether the flies and the smell of raw sewage in the small ditches running alongside the front of the homes bugged me as much as they did now.

Turning a corner, I saw the house come into the distance, the farm land in front of it looked the same as it always did, at least that was one thing. The oppressive heat and smell started taking its toll and I started to realise I was sweating profusely. Dragging the suitcase behind me as its wheels got stuck in ruts and cracks didn't help. I just realised I hadn't drunk any water since I had landed and was now starting to feel extremely thirsty.

I stopped in front of the house and looked up at it. A faded shadow of what it once was. Like everything else in the village. What was left had its colour faded with no one bothering to freshen it up. The blue metal gate had begun to rust and peel. The green mesh windows now turned to black with speckles of their old colour.

I saw a padlock on the gate, meaning Abbas had left and locked it from the outside. Had he forgotten I was coming?

The wicket gate on the home next door creaked open, a hand reached out and dropped a sack on the ground. I walked over and peered inside and saw it was an elderly man with a long grey beard with a line of sacks ready to take outside.

'Asalaam alaikum,' I said to him.

'Walaikum salaam,' the old man looked up at me to respond but continued to throw the sacks outside.

'Is Abbas home?'

'Khan saab? His mother in law is in hospital, I assume he's taken the wife and children to go see her.'

I waited a moment hoping to get some more information, but nothing came. I moved back to the door wondering what I could do. The old man stopped and peered out from the gate inquisitively.

'Are you Salim Khan?'

'Yes.'

The man's face lit up and his eyes widened.

'*Arrey yaar*, you don't recognise me?'

I looked at him and for some reason tried to imagine him without the beard and grey hair. Then I realised I needed to add a few extra pounds. It couldn't be.

'Munny?'

'Khan saab! Munny has been dead for years. I'm his eldest.'

Munny's son, the one who had gone to fight in Afghanistan. He would have been around the same age as me but he seemed a lot older.

'I'm sorry I didn't recognise you. It's just, I hope you don't mine me saying, I thought we were around the same age but you look older.'

He gave out a hearty laugh which made him sound almost like his father.

'Maybe it's the beard?' he asked with an almost toothless smile. 'I was sick for a while last year and it made me really weak, perhaps that's why I look older!'

'I'm sorry.'

'It's OK Khan saab,' he shook his head in a way as if to say he knew he was making me uncomfortable but didn't want me to feel so.

'When did you move next door?' I asked him. 'Was it Sarfraz saab who was living here before?'

'Yes, he died many years ago, your mother bought the house from his children as they had all moved to Islamabad and had no need for it. Then she let me rent it from her, and now I pay the rent to your brother.' He pondered for a moment. 'Thinking about it, that means half this house is your inheritance, I'm a bit late on the rent this month, but inshallah I'll have it next month when I sell these sugar canes,' he gestured at the sacks surrounding them.

At first I thought he was joking, but the solemnness on his face made me realise he was being absolutely serious.

'No *yaar*, I'm not here to pick up your rent!'

'I know that. But once you sort out your mother's inheritance with Abbas saab then I will pay you your half of the rent directly if you like.'

I couldn't believe what he was saying, as if I had come all this way after so long just for money and land.

'No I don't care for it. Just give the rent to Abbas, maybe I can convince him to half it for you seeing as I don't need my share.'

'Khan saab, what are you talking about? Haven't you come back to sort out your inheritance?'

I felt a mixture of anger and disappointment. Did he really think that low of me? But given the fact I had been away so long, how could he think anything else about me? Isn't that the only reason why most people would come back after so much time?

'I didn't come back for my inheritance. I came back because I wasn't here when I should have been.'

Solemnness clouded his face.

'I didn't mean to offend Khan saab. Forgive me.'

'It's OK, forget it, please.'

There was a brief momentary silence as he looked at my suitcase.

'Come inside please, have some rest until Abbas saab comes back. There must have been an emergency for him to leave all of a sudden.'

'I want to visit my mother's grave,' I interrupted him.

'You don't want to sit down and have a glass of water first?'

My sweaty tired condition must have been obvious.

'I came to visit her. I'd like to do that first.'

'Oh. They buried madam in the fields underneath the orange tree,' he pointed to the distance towards the lone tree in the middle of the fields around half a kilometre away. It had grown to a huge size since last I had seen it. 'She is next to your father and grandfather's graves. We buried my father there as well. Do you remember it?'

'Yes, thank you. Seeing someone familiar from my past after so long has really made me happy after so much sadness in the last few days.'

He gave a childish smile that reminded me of his father.

'My father always said, life was never the same since you left Khan saab. I'm glad you've come back, even if it is for a short while. Go, before the sun gets too hot. I will take your bags in and let my son know they are yours, you can pick them up when you come back.'

'Thank you.'

I walked back down the way I came, my crunching footsteps following me, until I found another dirt path to the left that led out into the fields. The last time I walked this way there were tall corn plantations on either side blocking the view of the horizon, now it was peppers growing low on the ground. I could see out into the distance all the other fields for miles around. After the short respite that was the conversation with Munny's son, I began to feel the punishing heat again, slowly becoming more and more intense as I kept walking on and the sun kept getting higher.

I started to feel dizzy, my shirt began to sag with sweat. I sat down on the side of the ditch to catch my breath. The sound of my footsteps were replaced with my heavy panting, and the sound of the constant buzzing of the heat now became apparent. A moment later a cool breeze began to blow, streaming over my face like cold water. Eventually my breathing eased after my short respite. I looked around and there wasn't a single other person to be seen in any direction. Of course not, it was coming close to the middle of the day, everyone had gone home to rest from the heat.

Another breath of wind blew from my left, for a moment it sounded like a whisper of someone's voice speaking. I looked up in the direction the wind came from and saw the orange tree in the distance. Three gravestones sat in a row, with another one separate from them. Munny's grave. The others were my father, grandfather and mother.

I began to realise this was the dream I had the day I received the letter from Ami.

I no longer felt the heat, but my forehead profused sweat that poured over my temples. I walked numbly towards what I had come all this way for, as I came closer I saw the grave closest had fresh soil on top, and as the writing on the grave came into view it was what I knew it would be, but somehow hoped it wouldn't.

"Amina Khan daughter of Iqbal Khan".

My legs gave way and I fell to my knees, shaking the dust into the air from beneath me. Tears now finally let themselves go and I felt all my pent-up anguish release itself. But now all I felt was emptiness. All the years of being away from her, a part of my life I had slowly let drip away, and before I realised it was now all gone.

'I'm sorry,' I said to her. Whether she could hear me or not, I couldn't care. 'I'm sorry for everything. Why did things have to be this way? Why couldn't you just accept what I had chosen for my life? Why did you have put all this grief on my shoulders?'

I sobbed like a baby and I didn't care. I didn't care about anything at that moment and at that time.

After I let go of all my emotions and all my grief, I stood

and my raised my palms facing towards me, and recited the opening chapter of the Qur'an. I prayed for her, my father, my grandfather and for Munny. I asked God to forgive them and me, to grant them a place in paradise. I had never asked God for anything with such conviction until this day.

As I wiped my palms over my face a voice came from behind me.

'Salim?'

I turned around and for a second thought I was looking in the mirror, but then realised I neither had a beard, nor was I wearing shalwar kameez. It was Abbas. We embraced and held each other in silence.

'I'm sorry Abbas. I left you and Ami.'

'It's OK brother,' he said handing me a handkerchief, though he also had tears running down his face. 'You're home now.'

'I'm too late. Too late for our mother.'

'She always remembered you Salim, she always thought of you. You never left her thoughts, it was like you were always with her.'

'She hated me Abbas. I know she did. I could feel it in her voice the few times we spoke.'

'She was like that with everyone. She always talked about you and remembered you. When I would mention you didn't write or visit she would always make excuses for you. She would say, "He must be busy with the family" or "He must be busy with the business". She never hated you. If I'm to be honest, I was always jealous of you. My big brother could get away with whatever he wanted and he would always have our mother's excuses.'

He let out a chuckle and so did I. It felt good to laugh.

I turned around to look at our mother's grave. Not knowing whether Abbas was just trying to make me feel better, but then I admonished himself for thinking my brother would lie to me. Now that I had come all this way I didn't know what do with myself.

'Salim, Ami left you something.' He rummaged through the side pocket in his kameez and handed me an envelope.

'What is it?'

'Ami left you a letter for when you came back. How she knew you would I don't know.'

'Why didn't you tell me about this before?' I said turning it over in his hands, the front of the envelope simply had "Salim" written in Urdu with a biro.

'She told me to only give it to you when you came here, and not to mention it to you before.'

I opened the envelope to see Ami's handwriting. The writing and the paper were the same as the letter she had sent telling me she had passed away.

"Salim, if you are reading this, then you would have received my first letter. Though I may not be able to tell you this in person before I die, I still wanted you to come to me after my death, it is the closest I can give to you as an apology in person. I'm sorry for what I did to you. I did the one thing a mother should never do, I denied you your happiness. After all these years with your wife and children I know now that I was wrong. I thought you would not be happy. But a few days ago Mawlana Ahmed called to tell me that Wasim was about to become a father. My own son who I remember nurturing as a small boy was now about to become a grandfather. The blessings Allah has given you from your marriage have never ceased. He gave us hindsight so that we may learn from our mistakes and grow from them, but my mistake pushed my son away from me. Every time I would talk to you I would remember my guilt of not approving of you marrying Linda. I'm sorry I couldn't tell this to you in person. But here in our home, in our land, in the place you grew up, I hope that you will forgive me, and that we will be together, all of us, in the next life. May God give you, Linda, Wasim and all your family happiness and goodness in this life and the one to come."

Now after all this time, I had finally found my peace. I now knew Ami didn't hate me, and she knew I didn't hate her, and it felt like we had both forgiven each other. This whole time I thought I had forgotten who I was and where I had come from, and with that I had forgotten about her. But Ami had never forgotten about me. For all these years there was a still a part of me living here as long as she remembered me. And though she was now gone, I had closed a chapter on my past which had kept me back from reclaiming a part of me. The regret I carried was now gone.

Abbas gently placed his hand on his shoulder.

'Welcome back home brother.'

ABOUT THE AUTHOR

Mohammed Khan

Mohammed was born and raised in London. A Son Returns is his first novel and is inspired by the stories of first generation migrants to Britain, like his father, who paved the way for many to call it "home". When he's not writing he's usually working as a software developer, and when he's not doing that he's reading, travelling or running. You can find his musings on many things via Instagram @britishmisk.

Printed in Great Britain
by Amazon